FIREHEART

JOHN G. HARTNESS

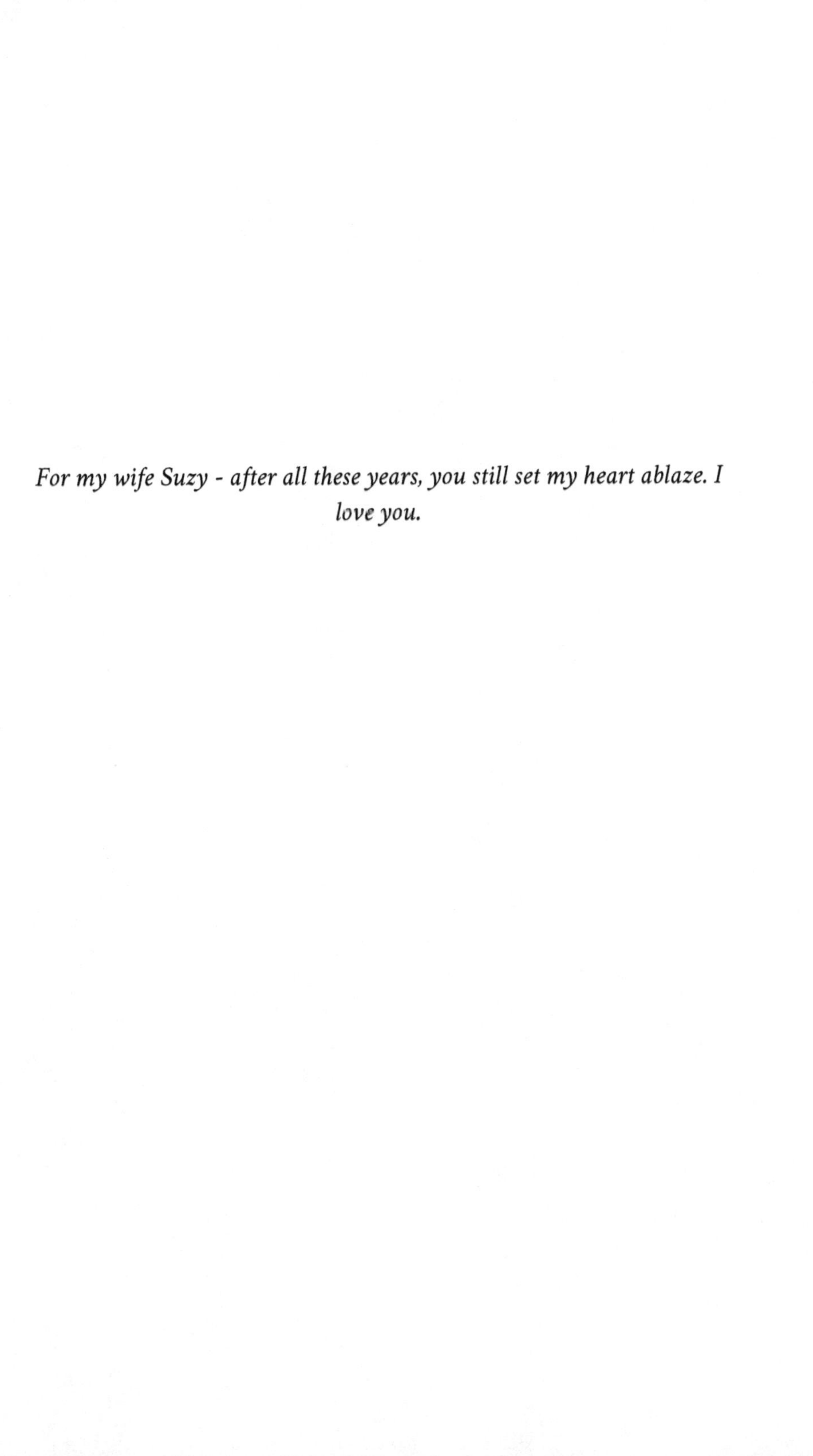

For my wife Suzy - after all these years, you still set my heart ablaze. I love you.

BEFORE

Hmmm? The great dragon opened one eye, but there was no light. He shrugged his giant shoulders, but the mountain pressed in all around him, hemming him in on all sides. He had just enough room to turn his head, just enough space in the cavern to breathe, but not enough room to stretch his gigantic body. *Why do I wake? What dares disturb the slumber of dragons?* He sent out his mind on fingers of magic, probing through layers of soil and rock, through roots and leaves, until finally he merged his consciousness with a bird flying high above his mountain. He pushed the bird aside, shunting the ignorant animal to the back of its puny brain, and saw. For the first time in thousands of years, he saw the sky, and the forest, and his mountain, and…men.

Men. He remembered men. Men were the reason for his self-imposed exile. Men were the reason he had not tasted fresh air for eons. Men were the reason his wings were stiff and penned in under the mountain. Men and their squalling spawn. Men and their fire. Men and their swords. Men and their numbers, growing faster than the land could support. And now, after so long, it was men who disturbed his slumber. Men and their machines. Men digging holes into *his* mountain.

Let them dig, he thought, pulling his awareness back into himself and letting the bird fly free across the mountain morning. He settled himself within his cavern and closed his eyes once more. *But woe be upon all mankind should they wake the others.*

CHAPTER 1

"Ow! Dammit! Ow! Dammit! Ow! Dammit!" It was like a mantra coming from the Hampton's second-floor bathroom. Rachel Hampton stood in front of the sink peering into the mirror with a critical eye and a pair of tweezers in one hand. She leaned in close to the glass, squinted one eye and darted in with the tweezers, grasping an offending hair close to the roots and yanking it out with a quick, painful tug.

"Ow! Dammit!" She leaned back in, searching the inch-wide landscape between her eyebrows for any more advance scouts in her war on unwanted facial hair. She slowly brought the tweezers to her face again, only to meet a new resistance. She looked up in the mirror and saw her father standing behind her, holding her elbow.

"That's enough torture for one morning, sweetheart. Put down the hot pincers and get some breakfast." Benjamin Hampton let go of his daughter's arm and stepped back, leaning against the doorjamb. "What are you doing, anyway? You keep that up and you won't have any eyebrows left."

"That would be a relief," Rachel muttered, dabbing at her brow with an alcohol-soaked cotton ball. "I've got this terrible unibrow growing in, and my moustache is going to be thicker than yours in a couple of weeks. I have got to start waxing that thing or I'm going to turn into one of those *Duck Dynasty* guys!"

Her father just laughed and pulled her into a hug. "I don't think any blond sixteen-year-old girl has to worry too much about a few tiny hairs nobody can even see. But since you're so perfect in every other way, I guess you've got to obsess over *something.* Now get dressed and come downstairs for breakfast."

Rachel looked down at her baggy cargo shorts and black Avett Brothers tank top and said, "What are you talking about? I am dressed." She saw the bewildered look on her father's face, laughed, and ducked past him into the hallway. She grabbed one of his flannel shirts off the banister, threw it on, and picked up her backpack from where it lay outside her bedroom door. She skipped down the stairs, and her father followed, shaking his head.

They sat down to a quick breakfast of corn flakes and bananas. Rachel made coffee for both of them, a job she took over almost ten years ago, just after her mom left. Her dad never admitted how awful the coffee was those first few years, but since getting to high school and starting to drink it herself, she had learned to brew a mean cup.

"So, what was all that torture in the mirror?" Ben asked. "You're already beautiful, so why the tweezers?"

"Yeah, right. Beautiful." Rachel didn't look up from her cereal.

"Who is he?"

"Who is who?" Rachel asked, still studying the rate of dissolution of corn flakes in milk.

"Whoever the boy is that you're literally pulling your hair out over."

"Why does there have to be a boy?"

"Okay, who's the girl? I'm a twenty-first century dad."

"Dad! I'm straight."

"Then we're back to my original question, aren't we?"

"And we're back to my original non-answer. His name is Nunya." She looked up at her father with one corner of her mouth twitching up.

He grinned right back at her, and they said in unison, "Nunya Business!" Ben laughed, and dropped it.

They ate in a comfortable silence for a few minutes, then Rachel asked, "What's going on at work today?"

Her dad didn't look up. "We're taking the top off Mount Creedy today."

There was a long silence, punctuated by the crunch of corn flakes, then Rachel finally said, "You know how awful that is, right?"

"It's not my favorite method of mining either, honey, but I'm here to do a job. And mountaintop removal is the most efficient way to get to the coal deposits in this part of the country. Once we move the overburden into the nearby valleys, there's more arable farmland than before, turning useless piles of rock into land that can actually be developed into something."

"I've heard the sales pitch, Dad, and I don't buy it. If it's such a great way to mine, why do we have to stay inside for gym class every time you guys are blasting?"

"That's just a precaution to make sure nothing happens. The danger is minimal. You're more likely to get struck by lightning than be injured by anything we're blasting. Anyway, nothing we say around the breakfast table is going to change a decision made by the suits in New York." Her father got up, took his bowl to the sink, and rinsed it out.

"Way to deflect, Pops. Blame the suits. You're the head geologist on this project. You could stop this if you really wanted to. But you don't care enough about our natural resources to do anything. Because you want the paycheck. Well done."

"You're right, Rachel. I do want a paycheck. Because I have to pay for this house, and this food, and those clothes, and your bike, and everything else around here! I want a paycheck because I have to take care of both of us, and I can't think about just myself, like a certain high school junior who is about to find herself grounded!" He took a deep breath, shook his head, and said, "I'm going to work now. If you need me, I'll be wantonly destroying the environment and twirling my moustache while shouting 'Bwa-Ha-Ha' at the defeated mountain."

Rachel slid off her barstool and put her dishes in the sink. "It's not funny, you know. This crap you're doing to the planet is going to come back and bite you in the ass someday."

Then she turned, grabbed her backpack, and headed out the side door to the garage. She unchained her silver Trek mountain bike from the wall, grabbed her helmet, and wheeled the bike out past her dad's beat-up white Ford Escape Hybrid with the Carson Creek Mining Company logo on the door. The irony of a coal company geologist driving a hybrid wasn't lost on her. She hopped on the bike and tightened the straps on her backpack. The three-mile route to Carson Creek High School was pretty tame, but she still didn't need thirty pounds of books to go flying out all over the highway as she rounded a turn. Again.

The ride to school gave Rachel a chance to clear her head and cool down a little after the argument with her dad. She knew he meant well, but the methods the mining company used were just so destructive. No matter how much they fought, she couldn't get him to see what she saw so clearly—that there's no way blowing the tops off mountains could possibly be good for the environment. But it was definitely good for the CEO's pockets and the shareholders' portfolios, and that's all anybody cared about anymore. Some days Rachel wished she lived in a bigger city instead of the little mountain town. Then she could pitch a tent on the city hall lawn and protest. She could pitch a tent here, of course, but people would just think she was camping.

Rachel was still a little lost in thought as she turned into the school parking lot, so she didn't see the taillights of the Mercedes until it was almost too late. The little coupe stopped short, and Rachel swerved hard to the left, right into the path of an oncoming pickup.

Brakes squealed, and Rachel pedaled hard to clear the front of the truck before it hit her, and she almost made it. The truck's front bumper just clipped her rear wheel, but it was enough to send Rachel flying sideways off the bike to land on the asphalt. Her head smacked the pavement, hard, and her bike helmet exploded into shards of plastic and Styrofoam. Her backpack dug painfully into her back, and she felt a sharp burning in her left knee that told her one more pair of jeans was probably done for.

Rachel lay in the parking lot for a few seconds trying to collect herself before she managed to sit up. She saw the tail of the Mercedes roll away, ignoring the carnage it left in its wake. She knew whose car it was, of course. Not many Mercedes convertibles in the student parking lot, so everybody knew it belonged to Jessica Baker, head cheerleader and all-around Queen Bee. But just as Rachel started to get a good internal monologue going about what a bitch Jessica was, she heard footsteps running toward her.

"Don't sit up. You might be really hurt." Rachel's heart fell into her stomach at the sound of a familiar voice.

Of course it's Scott Morrison's truck that I swerved in front of. Because the universe really does hate me. Please tell me it's the thirteenth. I know it's not Monday, but it's totally NOT my lucky day. Rachel sagged back to the pavement, wishing she could sink through it into the ground. When the ground steadfastly refused to open and swallow her, she struggled up to her knees and tried to stand. Her left leg buckled under her, though, and Scott hurried forward to catch her before she fell.

"Hey! You really shouldn't be standing." She looked up at his brown eyes, full of concern, and her knees went weak all over again. Scott helped her back to a sitting position on the ground and started to look her over for injuries.

"Are you all right?" he asked. "You seem a little...I don't know. Did you hit your head?"

"No, I'm fine," Rachel replied. "My helmet did its job. I think I've got a little road rash on one knee. Just help me up, and I'll be fine." *As long as I don't smell your cologne or look in those eyes again.*

"Are you sure? Holy shit! You're bleeding!" He pointed at her left knee, and sure enough, the fabric was shredded and soaked with blood.

"It's not a big deal," she said, trying to wave off the gathering crowd. "Just a little scratch. Don't worry about it. It was totally my fault." She saw Scott look at her out of the corner of one eye and held up her hands. "No, really! Look, you didn't even bend the wheel of my bike. Much. Shit." When she looked closer, she could see that the wheel was just enough out of true that she wouldn't be able to ride it until she got it fixed.

"Look, I'll take care of the bike. I promise," Scott said. "And I'll give you a ride home today. You're Ben Hampton's daughter, right? Your dad works with my dad. I think I know where you live. I'll take you home after school, then give you a ride to the bike shop and pay for the wheel. Okay?" It was more than okay with Rachel, who was getting a fluttery feeling in her stomach at the thought of that much time with Scott Morrison. *Maybe today won't be a total suck-fest after all.*

Then a tall boy stepped up and shoved Scott right in the chest, and the day returned to its normal level of terrible. "What the hell do you think you're doing, Morrison?" Billy Preston shoved Scott again and got right up in his face. "You think your rich daddy's going to get you out of this one? I saw the whole thing, total reckless driving. And I'm going to make sure this doesn't get swept under the rug like everything else you pull."

Scott looked bewildered for a minute, then recovered and shoved Billy back. "My dad doesn't have anything to do with this, Billy. I didn't do anything wrong here. She rode out in front of me, and I'm just trying to make it right, even though it's not my fault."

"Not your fault? If you'd been paying attention to what was around you instead of trying to stare down Jessica Baker's shirt, you might have seen Rachel coming!" Scott blushed at this, but said nothing.

Billy kept going. "You company guys, you're all alike. You think you can do anything you want to the normal people around here. Well, not this time, Scotty-boy. This time you screwed up and ran down a girl on her bike, and I'm gonna make sure they yank your license for it!"

Scott tried to reach out for Billy again, but Rachel was there between them. "Stop this, both of you!" She turned to Billy. "Scott's right, Billy. He didn't do anything. *I* was the one not paying enough attention. I didn't see Jessica hit her brakes until too late, and I swerved in front of Scott's truck. It wasn't his fault, and he was very nicely offering to fix my wheel before you came and stuck your nose in. Now would you please go to class? I'm fine."

Billy grumbled something else about "rich kids" under his breath and turned to walk across the parking lot to the school.

Rachel turned back to Scott. "Sorry about that. Billy's been my best friend since my mom…well, for years, and sometimes he gets protective."

"And he hates my father," Scott said quietly. He watched Billy walk into the school building, then turned those deep brown eyes back on Rachel.

"But that's got nothing to do with me. Or you. So, um, if you still want that ride home, the offer's still open. And I'll still take care of your bike. If you want me to, I mean. I wouldn't want you to have to take charity from a company guy, after all." The bitter smile on his face said he'd heard that phrase a lot.

"I think my head geologist father kinda counts as a company man, too, Scott. And I'll be happy to take your charity, I mean, your ride, I mean…I'm going to stop talking now." Rachel turned away and picked up her backpack and the remnants of her helmet.

"I guess I owe you a bike helmet, too. That one looks trashed," Scott said. He picked up her bike and put it into the bed of his Silverado.

"They're made to shatter like that on impact. It keeps the kinetic energy from transferring to your skull. So yeah, I'll pick up a new one at Bike World this afternoon. But you're not paying for it. I should accept some responsibility for my actions. At least that's what my dad keeps telling me."

"Yeah, mine too. So I'll see you after school?" Scott said.

"It's a date. I mean, it's not a *date*, but it's a…I'm going back to not talking now." Rachel felt her cheeks turning a darker red than the blood on her knee and turned away so Scott wouldn't see.

"It can be a date," Scott said quietly. "We can get pizza after. I'll meet you at my truck after school."

"Okay," Rachel said, then hurried up the hill to the school, not trusting herself to say anything else.

She started down the hall to English class, then made a sharp turn into the girls' bathroom to try and take care of the worst of her bloody knee, which had slowed to a trickle. Of course, the voice that greeted her upon walking into the bathroom was the one she least wanted to hear: Jessica Baker.

"I swear, it was like I looked up in my rearview mirror and just went crazy. I saw that granola girl riding her silly mountain bike, and I was a woman possessed. I just slammed on my brakes and sent her flying! It was awesome!"

"Yeah, it was awesome, Jessica. Thanks for wrecking my bike and almost getting me killed. I really think you're just the *best*," Rachel said, shouldering her way past Jessica and her gaggle of bleach-blond idiot friends to get to the sink. She pulled her ripped jeans away from her knee and winced as the denim came free of her bloodied skin.

"Ewwww!" Jessica said, looking at the blood. "Do you have to do that *here*? Why can't you go to the nurse like a normal person?"

Rachel whirled on the pretty blonde and grabbed her blouse with one blood-stained hand. She pulled Jessica close and growled, "If some dizzy bitch with more money than brains hadn't decided it would be fun to make me crash my bike, I wouldn't have to do this anywhere. As it is, I'm bleeding all over the place, the nurse can't even give me an aspirin, and I have an essay test first period that I can't miss. So if you'll *excuse me*, Miss Reckless Driver, I'm going to try to get my knee to stop bleeding before class starts." Rachel let go of the other girl and gave her a little shove backward.

Jessica looked down at her ruined blouse and hissed, "You will pay for this, you little tramp. This blouse was expensive. I had to order it!"

"I'm sure, since there aren't any stores in town snotty enough for you. Now leave me alone before I bleed on something else of yours." Rachel grabbed a wad of paper towels and wet them in the sink, then cleaned her knee the best she could while standing on one leg in the bathroom. She could hear Jessica and the others leaving the room, but she couldn't bring herself to care.

"I have a date with Scott Morr-i-son," she sang under her breath as she picked tiny bits of gravel out of her knee and washed most of the blood out of her pants leg. The last bell rang, and she hurriedly scrubbed her hands and threw the bloody mess of paper towels away as she ran out the door to her English class.

Morning classes were uneventful. The essay in English was mostly painless, and even the pop quiz in trig wasn't terrible. It wasn't until gym class that the crushing suck of high school returned with a vengeance. Because of the scheduled blasting and the potential for debris, all outside activities were cancelled.

That meant one thing for gym class: dodgeball. Rachel usually didn't hate dodgeball, but her bum leg was going to slow her down and make her a target for Jessica and her bitchy friends, plus any jock boys who wanted to impress her, which would be all of them. So, it was with no small amount of dread that she changed into shorts and a t-shirt and headed into the gym to join the rest of the class. Coach McSwain was waiting for them in his standard ensemble of nothing but school colors: white knee socks, crimson shorts, black polo shirt, and gleaming silver whistle. He looked almost like a caricature of a high school coach, except that he saw nothing at all ironic in the way he dressed. He had never been seen not wearing school colors, and it was rumored that he even got married in a black tuxedo with a crimson cummerbund.

"Rachel, what happened to your leg?" Coach asked as Rachel limped onto the basketball court.

"I fell on my bike this morning." She exaggerated her limp a little in hopes that he would take pity on her and let her out of dodgeball.

No such luck. "Well, way to be a trooper and push through the pain, girly. Good going. For that, you get to be one of the captains today. Now, who wants to be the other team captain?"

It came as no surprise when Jessica raised her hand and skipped over to Coach's side. Rachel somehow managed not to groan and waved for Jessica to pick first.

"I pick Amanda," Jessica said in a sing-song voice, calling over her best friend and one of Rachel's bathroom tormentors. Amanda skipped over to her BFF's side, her perfect auburn curls bouncing almost as much as her giant boobs.

"Rachel, it's your turn," Coach McSwain said.

"Billy, get over here," Rachel said. Billy trotted over to her side with a grin. At least she had one friend on her team.

"Jessica." Coach pointed to her.

"I take Aaron." Amanda bounced up and down with glee at her friend's selection of the starting quarterback, starting pitcher, and basically starting everything for the school's athletics teams. He also happened to be Amanda's boyfriend, just to complete the cliché.

"Give me Belinda," Rachel said. Belinda was a good athlete, but with her dad being the town's best plumber, her roots were too ordinary for her to make Jessica's team.

"I want Wilson," Jessica said, taking the almost seven-foot-tall center for the basketball team.

"Give me Anders." Rachel took the German exchange student who spent every break between classes sneaking cigarettes behind the dumpster and scowling at everyone.

Team selection went like that until everyone in the class was lined up beside one of the two captains. Predictably, Jessica's team was all the beautiful people: the jocks, the cheerleaders, the one or two smart kids with enough social skills to float on the edges of cool. Rachel's team had one or two people who flirted with acceptability in high school society, like Billy, but mostly it was misfits, smart kids, and losers. Rachel thought of them as "her people."

Coach McSwain handed out the red rubber balls that Rachel thought of as more torture devices than exercise aids, and her team immediately saw three casualties as Aaron, Wilson, and their friend Jake all launched perfect strikes at various kids they loved to torment. Rachel ducked a ball Jessica flung right at her face and responded by grabbing a rolling red orb of pain and humiliation and flinging it at Amanda. The ball caught the bouncy redhead in the center of her chest and rebounded harder than Mandy's last boyfriend. The pretty girl flounced to the side as Jessica glared at Rachel.

From there the game devolved into a full-scale war of cool kids versus the misfits, with the cool kids predictably coming out on top. Rachel watched her team shrink as nerds, goths, stoners, and freaks all fell to the barrage of well-aimed balls pitched by the jocks, the rich kids, the pretty girls, and of course, Jessica. Before the period was half over, Billy and Rachel were the last two players on their team, standing side by side against eight of the best athletes in the school. With a grin, Aaron and Wilson cocked their arms back, and the whole opposing team sent balls flying in Rachel and Billy's direction. Pelted from every angle, they left the court, battered and with bright red marks on their arms and faces from the impact, as the pretty people celebrated another victory over the underprivileged and under-beautified.

"Well, that sucked about as much as I thought it would," Rachel said, sitting on the bleachers beside Billy.

"I dunno," Billy demurred, "I kinda liked watching Jessica jump around in that tight t-shirt."

"Don't let Aaron hear you say that," Rachel warned. "He'll break your ass."

"He can kiss my ass," Billy said, not before he looked around to make sure Aaron wasn't within earshot.

Rachel opened her mouth for a retort, but the words froze on her lips as a thunderous *BOOM* shook the room. She turned to Billy, who was already standing and running to the top of the bleachers, the only place in the gym where students could see out the windows. She followed him, injured knee and all, concern for her father making her forget her pain for a few minutes.

A huge cloud of smoke and ash billowed into the sky from what used to be the top of Mount Creedy, one of the richest sources of coal Morrison Mining Co. had ever discovered. No matter how much she hated the thought of mountaintop removal mining, she knew that the seam they uncovered today would keep her father in work for several years to come.

Regardless, she hated the process and hated the thought of her father being up there when the explosives went off even more. She knew she shouldn't be worried. *He is a geologist,* she kept telling herself, *not an explosives technician or a miner.* But she couldn't help it. Whenever there was a big blast, she worried all day until he got home, and if he had to work late, she would ride her bike over the hill to the mine and bug the gate guards until she could see for herself that he was safe.

But this was the biggest blow they'd ever done, and she couldn't help but worry that something was going to go wrong and her dad was in trouble.

CHAPTER 2

The noise and shock rumbling through the earth yanked the great dragon from his semi-somnolent state to full consciousness in an instant.

What is this? the giant golden beast thought. *Do these men dare destroy my lair? What have they done?* The dragon flexed his giant shoulders and felt the dirt and pebbles shifting above him. After all these years, he was no longer trapped beneath the hillside. Somehow, these foolish humans had found a way to take the entire top off the mountain, revealing his broad golden back to the sun.

He couldn't move, his wings, neck, and tail still trapped under tons of rock, but one concentrated mental blast took care of that, blasting granite, shale, and coal twenty feet into the air in all directions. The dragon shook himself all over and stretched, s-t-r-e-t-c-h-e-d, his tail and neck for the first time in thousands of years. His long hibernation had left him weak, but his magic, tied so deeply to the power of the land, was still strong. He lifted his gigantic head up, up, up past the enormous crater these stupid little men had created with their explosions and looked around. All manner of machines and structures were scattered around his mountaintop. At least, they were scattered around what had been his mountaintop. Now there was just a big hole where once majestic pines had grown, rubble where once proud fingers of stone reached for the clouds.

The dragon's head slowly rose above the edge of the crater, and for the first time since druids walked these woods, he found himself face to face with a man. This man seemed somehow less than those he had known in his day, weaker and more fragile. Still, the habits of a lifetime die hard, and dragons are a decorous lot, so the dragon knew it was his place, as the greater being, to speak first.

"Hello, little manling. I am Auros the Gold. It is pleasing to me to once again feel sunlight on my scales."

The little man was obviously stupid, for he did not respond. At least, not in words. He screamed like a slaughtered sheep and pulled a strange tube from his belt and pointed it at Auros. The tube made several strange popping sounds, and Auros felt a painful stinging sensation on his nose. He shook his head to drive away the insect, but the little man kept making his tube pop, and the dragon's nose stung more and more.

Finally, the dragon lost his patience with the little man and bellowed "STOP!" punctuating his roar with a small lick of flame at the man's feet. It was just a tiny tongue of fire, not enough to do more than singe the hair on the man's legs, if he had any hair underneath those strange leggings, but he screamed like a sheep again and danced backward, falling down the side of the mountain for several feet until he fetched up against a boulder and lay still.

Auros crawled farther out of the crater, using his forelegs for purchase in the loose soil and rock as his twenty-foot tail finally pulled free of the crater and flicked around his haunches. After several minutes of scrambling to the lip of the hole, the dragon was finally free. Free, after many years of confinement. Free to hunt, free to explore the new land of men, free to stretch his wings and take to the skies again after so long.

But first, he must understand why these men woke him, and he must make sure they dig no farther, lest they wake the others. Auros peered down the side of the mountain to the mass of humans below, trying to discern from their garb who was their leader.

Finally, he decided to simply fly down and ask the men. He spread his giant golden wings, forty feet wide tip to tip, and unfurled his spiked tail into the air. He gave a mighty flap of his wings and pushed off from the ground with his magic. Auros soared into the air and rolled twice, shaking the worst of the dirt from his scales. *I must bathe soon,* he thought. *It would be unseemly to hold an audience with their king in such a state of disarray.*

He landed in front of a clump of men who seemed amazed to see him, or perhaps they were struck dumb by his majesty. They gaped like village idiots at the dragon, and he feared that he had been awakened by a tribe of morons, not that humans at their best were the intellectual equals of dragons. Nonetheless, he resolved to speak to them with respect, even if they proved themselves fools.

"I am Auros the Gold. Who among you speaks for your king?"

The men said nothing and merely cowered behind their strange yellow carriages with giant wheels and pointed more tubes at him. One man stepped forward, empty hands in the air above his head. Auros recognized the gesture—the man meant no harm. Auros responded in kind by lowering his head almost completely to the ground and looking the man in the eye. His eye was the size of the man's head, and the man did not seem reassured by Auros' gesture of peace.

"I am Ben Hampton. W-what are you?" the man asked.

Auros heard the sounds coming from the man, but he spoke no language that Auros knew. Could the world have changed so much in such short a time? Since it was obvious that this human did not speak Dragon, he tried his question again in Elvish, Dwarven, and even Trollish. The last caused the human to duck and take several steps back, as Trollish was a nasty, brutish language not fit for civilized species.

After trying to no avail to communicate with the human in all the languages he knew, Auros finally roared his frustration and shook his head at the human. The man danced back, and one of the men behind him raised his tube. Fire sparked from the tube, and a sudden pain erupted in Auros' shoulder.

The dragon whipped his neck around to see a thin trickle of blood dripping from between his neck and shoulder scales. He whirled on the man with the tube and opened his mouth wide. He focused his magic, and a thin tendril of flame licked out and enveloped the man, burning him to ash where he stood. The tube clattered to the ground, and the man in front of him turned and ran behind another of the strange yellow carriages.

"Think not to harm Auros the Gold, humans! I am your ally. I do not wish to destroy you, but I will not be attacked in such a manner!" The dragon sat up on his rear legs and haunches, raising his head some fifty feet above the terrified men.

The men below him panicked, and they aimed their weapons at him and opened fire. Bullets filled the air, buzzing like angry wasps, and Auros felt dozens of painful stings as the tiny projectiles found the vulnerable spaces between scales and the tender membrane of his wings. The dragon summoned more magic, and a great gout of flame sprang from his mouth as he swept his head back and forth, setting men and carriages on fire. The shooting stopped, replaced with the screams and cursing of men and dragon alike. Auros spread his wings, shoved against the ground below him with his magic, and took to the sky.

More bullets bounced off his solid belly scales, and the dragon swept across the edge of the crater with his massive tail. Men dove for cover, and rocks and dirt poured into the crater that had once held the dragon, re-sealing the cavern from the humans. Auros beat his mighty wings and flew, spraying fire over the men below as he made his escape. The men screamed and ran to hide behind their carriages, but the fire rained down over them, setting their clothes alight and turning them into little running bonfires. Auros felt a moment of pity for them, then turned his face to the sky.

Do not try to hunt a dragon, little men. It does not end well for your kind.

It felt good to fly again after so many years asleep. Auros began to awaken muscles long dormant and stretched to his full hundred-foot length as he flew over what had once been his valley. The valley was very different now, but that was to be expected. As he had predicted, men were everywhere, thicker than ants and spread across his valley. The great trees he had known were gone, and the mountains were hemmed in by pastures and fields. That was the problem with men— they always felt the need to change the land to fit them, instead of changing themselves to fit the land.

He flew, his eyes scanning the horizon for any hint of familiarity in this world, finding nothing. He flew over wide paths carved through the mountains, over villages larger than any he remembered humans capable of building, and logged many changes in this world. He flew, and as he flew, a rumble from his stomach reminded him of a primal need. *I hunger.* It had been many, many years since he had hunted, and now that his hibernation was over, the hunger was almost more than he could bear. Auros flew lower, peering through the trees for deer or moose, but saw nothing.

I must hunt in another form. He flew lower still and drew his wings in tight to his body. He furled his tail close to his haunches and landed in a small clearing in a forest near a cluster of the giant huts that men of this land seemed to favor. The dragon settled onto all fours in the center of the clearing and drew his magic around him. The magic was strong here, and Auros could feel it flow from the soil and the trees, from the grass and the animals. Every living thing gave a part of itself to the magic, and the land here was rich with it. He felt the dappled swirl of the sunlight on his scales and spun the magic into himself.

He cast a mental picture of his chosen form and poured himself into it. He could feel his body shrinking, shifting, molding to fit the new form in his mind. He felt the twigs beneath him poke his newly tender skin as his scales vanished, and he wobbled on two legs as his tail disappeared. His hair, something he had not worn in centuries, fell into his eyes and obscured his vision, already reduced by the restraints of this new form. After a few moments, the magical light surrounding him faded, and where an enormous dragon had once sat, a perfectly formed human male now stood, with golden hair, a yellowish tinge to his skin, and brilliant green eyes.

Auros looked down at his new form and found it pleasing. He had remembered all the fingers and toes, and he looked behind him to confirm that, yes, his tail was indeed gone. *Much better*, he thought. *This form will require less food as well.*

He sent his thoughts out, seeking food, and found a deer grazing nearby. It was a male, and an adult, so he felt no remorse in calling it to him. The deer came through the trees a few moments later, and Auros raised a hand to it. Power flew from his fingertips and struck the animal, killing it instantly. Auros staggered; he was weaker than he thought. Foregoing his usual manners, he walked to the deer and ripped off a hind leg. He held up the leg, furrowed his brow, and focused his magic. In seconds, the skin and hair of the leg were burned completely off, leaving a charred hunk of moderately cooked meat.

It is not as I would have done at my best, but it will suffice. The dragon sat cross-legged on the ground and began to rip hunks of the smoldering flesh from the bone and shove it in his mouth. The grease and blood ran down his chin in steaming rivulets as he crammed mouthfuls of the delicious meat into himself. It had been so long since he last ate, he almost forgot to chew, but eventually half the leg of deer was gone and his belly was swollen with meat. Exhausted from his awakening and the exertions, Auros curled himself into a ball on the soft leaves of the forest floor and went to sleep with his head resting on the deer's carcass.

As he slept, he dreamt of other dragons. The dreams were not pleasant.

CHAPTER 3

Rachel was just stepping out of the shower in the girls' locker room when the PA crackled to life. "All students please report to the gymnasium for an emergency assembly. Please do not run in the halls. The assembly will begin in fifteen minutes. Please do not leave any personal belongings in your classrooms. This is a mandatory assembly."

The girls all looked at each other, then began dressing quickly. At Carson Creek High, an emergency assembly only meant one thing: an accident at the mine. More than two-thirds of the students had family working there, and the rest of the families in town worked in some support capacity, at shops or restaurants. Years had passed since the last major accident, but everyone remembered what it felt like.

Even Jessica wasn't bitchy about the assembly, like she usually was when there was anything in the gym that didn't involve her wearing her cheerleading uniform. She looked pale as she sat on a bench tying her shoes, and Rachel went over to put a hand on her shoulder.

"I'm sure he's fine, Jess," Rachel said. She knew Jessica's parents. Her dad was the first shift foreman and worked closely with her father. Rachel knew she was probably just as ashen as Jessica—if anything really bad happened at the mine, both of their fathers were possibly hurt or worse.

"Thanks," the other girl replied without looking up. "Sorry about this morning. I was a stupid bitch."

"It happens. Don't worry about it," Rachel said. She went to her locker and threw on her street clothes and slid into her tennis shoes. She didn't bother with trying to make her hair do anything, just yanked it back into a ponytail and tossed everything into her gym bag. She was out the locker room door and halfway to the gym less than two minutes after the announcement.

She walked into the gym amid the buzz of worried conversation and scanned the bleachers for Billy. No matter what an ass he'd been earlier, he was still her best friend, and if anything…well, if there was bad news, he was the guy she wanted to be with when she heard it. But she didn't see him anywhere, and then a hand took her by the elbow and guided her to a pair of open seats.

"It's not exactly as romantic as getting your bike tire fixed, but can we call this a first date?" She looked up into Scott's brown eyes, and even her good knee went a little weak.

She tried to recover by laughing at his dumb joke and sitting down where he indicated. "It can count as a date, but you'd better not think I'm letting you get to second base."

Scott laughed and held up both hands. "I'll keep them to myself, I swear. At least here." He mumbled that last part, and Rachel hit him in the shoulder. She caught sight of Billy just then and waved him over. He squeezed in on the bleacher beside Rachel and nodded to Scott.

"You know what's going on, rich boy?"

"I don't know any more than you do, Billy. I hope everything's okay."

"It's not," Billy said. "They never call us in here if everything's okay. If it's no big deal, like somebody broke an arm or a leg, they don't tell us anything until we get home. If somebody's dead, they come get you out of class. But if there's an assembly? It's bad." Billy put his elbows on his knees and his chin in his palms.

"How do you know so much?" Scott asked before Rachel could stop him.

Billy looked over at him like he'd just asked the rudest, most ridiculous question on Earth, then relaxed a little. "I forget you just got here last year. It seems like forever. My brother died in a collapse a couple years ago. They pulled me out of French class. I never did learn how to conjugate *conduire*."

"I'm sorry," Scott said after a minute. Rachel could see the reality sinking in for Scott, the fear that his classmates lived with every day.

"Thanks." Billy turned back to watching the microphone sitting in the middle of the basketball court. No administrators were anywhere in sight as the gym filled with students. After what seemed like way more than fifteen minutes, the guidance counselor, Mrs. Hardin, walked out to the microphone.

"Oh shit, this must be really awful if they sent the counselor out to make the announcement," Billy muttered.

Mrs. Hardin, a stout woman in her fifties, was the guidance counselor and women's volleyball coach. She wore almost the same outfit as Coach McSwain, only a slightly more feminine polo shirt with the school's lion mascot over her left breast. She tapped the microphone with one finger, and a squeal of feedback cut through the gym speakers.

She leaned down and spoke into the microphone. "Ahem. Um. May I have your attention, please? There has been an incident at the mine this morning. Several mine security workers have been injured. At this time, we have no further information, but we are asking all students to remain calm. If you have a parent or sibling working first shift mine security, please see Mr. Fernwood immediately, and he will allow you to be dismissed from school. As I said, we have no further information at this time, but please—"

A scream from the top bleachers cut her off. "It's a monster! There's a monster at the mine and it's killing people!" All heads turned to Allyson Hough, who was staring at her cell phone screen and shrieking.

"Calm down. Please return to your seats. Miss Hough, please bring me your cell phone this instant." Mrs. Hardin stood at the microphone tapping her foot, but the students ignored her, swarming Allyson to catch a glimpse of whatever she was looking at.

"I uploaded it to Facebook," Allyson announced, and all eight hundred students and teachers reached into pockets and purses and logged onto the social networking site to view the video. Those few without a smartphone or tablet looked over the shoulders of those who did.

Rachel turned to Billy, who had pulled out his iPad at the first mention of Facebook and had the video running across the screen. Rachel watched in horror as her father confronted the dragon, then dove behind a truck to avoid a blast of fire from the monster's mouth. She recognized Edward Stephenson, the first man killed by the dragon. He had been to their house for dinner once or twice and sometimes sat on the porch drinking beer and talking about different types of coal with her father. He'd been in the mining business since he dropped out of high school at fifteen and worked the seams until he was too old to go down into the mountain anymore. Then he'd made the switch to security and mostly spent his time checking IDs at the gate and signing off on shipping manifests.

Except now he was dead, fried to cinders by what looked like a...*dragon?* That didn't make any sense. Rachel shook her head and reached over Billy's shoulder, tapping the screen to rewind the video. Sure enough, it looked like a dragon. Huge lizard-looking thing— wings, tail, breathing fire. If there was a dragon-building checklist, this thing seemed to have all the right parts.

Rachel felt movement beside her and turned as Scott stood up and started walking toward the gym doors. She hopped up and went after him, Billy hot on her heels, reaching for his tablet. "Where are you going?" she asked as she caught up to Scott just before Mrs. Hardin cut him off at the door.

"I was going to ask you the very same question, Mr. Morrison. I know for a fact that neither of your parents are on first shift security, so you can return to your class now." The guidance counselor was built like a fullback and didn't look inclined to move.

"No, he's not, but my father will be on his way to the mine right now, and he'll want me there with him. He's teaching me how to handle crises, and I think digging up a dragon and getting a bunch of your men killed counts as a crisis," Scott answered her.

"And he's my ride. At least he is since he wrecked my bike this morning." Rachel pointed to Scott, who looked down at her sharply, and she shrugged. "Well, you kinda did, anyway."

"What about you, Mr. Preston? What is your reason that I should allow you to just randomly leave the premises?" Mrs. Hardin glared at the third member of their trio.

"I was really just trying to get my iPad back, but since that was my uncle Edward that we all just watched get roasted like a goddamn marshmallow, I think I'm going to go take care of my mom whether you like it or not."

Mrs. Hardin gasped and took a step back, her hand flying to her mouth. "I'm sorry, William. I had no idea he was a relation. Of course, the three of you go right along. And William, please take all the time you need. Family comes first at a time like this."

The three teens pushed past the guidance counselor and into the hall, making their way quickly to the parking lot. Scott's truck was a four-door, so they piled in the cab, and he pulled out of the parking lot onto the road leading to the mine.

After driving in silence for a few seconds, Scott leaned forward and said, "I'm sorry about your uncle, Billy. I didn't know."

"Yeah, me either," added Rachel.

"That makes three of us," Billy replied, looking spectacularly unlike someone who has just watched a relative get incinerated.

"What?" Rachel turned to face Billy.

"I made that up. I knew Ed, of course. Everybody knew Ed. And he was an awesome dude, but he didn't have any family. He told me that one time when I was working the loading dock over the summer."

"So you lied to Mrs. Hardin?" Rachel asked.

"Seriously, Rache, I'm sixteen. Lying to adults is what I do. And there's no way I'm gonna let you two dorks go off chasing a dragon without me. It's like the world's biggest *Dungeons & Dragons* game."

"Only you don't get to re-roll a character if you get killed," Scott said.

"I'm going to ignore the fact that you're both speaking fluent Geek and just say that I don't plan on getting killed. Now drive faster," Rachel said.

They pulled up to the gates of the mine less than ten minutes after leaving the school. The security guard at the gate held up his hand to stop them, then stepped aside when he recognized Scott in the driver's seat. Scott pulled the truck up beside the man and rolled down the window.

"What happened, Brady?"

"Mr. Morrison, good to see you. I don't rightly know, to be honest with you. I'm a second-shift guy and was asleep when the call came down from your father to get up here and help out manning the gate. Seems like there was some kind of secondary explosion from this morning's blast that got a couple guys injured, and maybe even a fatality. I think Ed might be the one killed, but I'm not real sure. I don't know anything for sure. Like I said, I was asleep when everything happened."

"Thanks, Brady. Will you radio my dad and let him know that I'm here and I need a couple of spare hard hats?"

"Will do, sir. Um…" The portly security guard hesitated, as if he didn't know how to say what he needed to say.

"What is it, Brady? You know anything you tell me is between you and me. My dad doesn't have to know about it if you don't want him to."

"It's not that, Mr. Morrison, it's just…well, some of the boys that were here, they're saying that it wasn't no explosion. They're saying it was some kind of monster come out of the ground and hurt all those folks. I don't really know what to make of that, is all."

"Well, Brady, I don't know any more than you do. After all, I just got here. But for now, if anybody asks, let's stick to the party line. And if I hear anything different, I'll let you know. How does that sound to you?"

"Sounds good, sir. I just wanted to know what to tell *them*." The disgust was thick in Brady's voice as he pointed back out the gate at the news vans that were already starting to set up across the road from the mine. The vans had taken up position in the same spots so often over the years for various cave-ins, accidents, protests, and announcements that some enterprising miner had painted lines on the gravel with the different stations' call letters, like a real parking lot. Now the news jockeys parked in their assigned spaces and actually got mad if someone jumped their spot.

Scott looked back over his shoulder and sighed. "They're fast, aren't they? Well, until we know something definite, let's say what my father told us to say and be honest about what we don't know. Nobody can string us up for being honest, can they?"

"No, sir. Thank you, Mr. Morrison."

"Thanks, Brady. I'll check back with you before we leave." Scott put the truck in gear and rolled slowly through the gate. Brady pulled the gate closed behind him and returned to his tiny guard hut.

"Where did you learn to work people like that?" Billy asked.

"What do you mean?" Scott replied.

"You had that dude eating out of your hand and calling you 'Mr. Morrison' like you're somebody. You're just a high school kid like the rest of us."

"No, I'm not. When I'm here, I'm the boss's son, the one who spends all summer going to meetings and holding his dad's clipboard, but I'm also the guy who makes it his business to know all the security guys and all the foremen personally because I know it won't be too long before they're all working for me. I'm coming back here after college, and if they remember me as being a good guy, it'll be easier for them to respect me then. It was tough on my dad when we first got here because he was the guy from out of town. But I won't be. I'll be the kid that grew up around the mine, went away to college, and came back. So, I treat everybody with respect, and they do the same to me."

"Isn't that a little cold, Morrison? Like that Machiavelli dude we were studying?"

"You say cold; I say practical. Tomato, to-mah-to."

Rachel just sat between the boys looking straight ahead out the windshield. Her dad didn't seem to be hurt in the video she'd seen, but that didn't show everything. He had to be okay, he just had to. She couldn't stand to think of anything happening to him.

The truck pulled up to the mine office, and Scott hopped out. He reached behind the seat and pulled out a battered hard hat and put it on.

"The whole mine is a hard hat area, so let me get you a couple before we go any farther." He walked over to the office and disappeared. He returned just a few seconds later with two bright pink hard hats. Billy and Rachel got out of the truck and took the hats.

"Cute," Rachel said, putting the hat on and adjusting the strap to fit her. Whoever wore the hat before her must have had a huge head.

"Why pink?" Billy asked, not looking nearly as taken as Rachel with the color.

"So people don't steal them. What kind of miner would want a pink hard hat?" Scott answered.

Rachel could see the logic but thought that the hat looked pretty good on her regardless. She gazed around the mine yard. It had been several months since she had last been to the mine with her father, and there hadn't been near this many vehicles or people around then. Ambulances and other emergency service vehicles were all clustered around the blast site, half a mile or more from where they stood at the mine office. The office and the company store were the only permanent structures at the site, low cinderblock buildings with nothing in the way of frills except one small window box that held a few scraggly daisies. Mrs. Ruth, the bookkeeper, tried her best to keep a little color around the place, but the daisies were perpetually coated with a thin layer of dark gray coal dust.

A large tent was set up beside the company store, in the parking lot where her dad's truck usually sat. From the array of ambulances and EMTs around the tent, Rachel guessed that it was the emergency field hospital that the county had bought with FEMA money the last time there was a mine collapse. It was a big green structure with walls on all sides, like something she'd seen in *M*A*S*H* reruns. There was even a big area cleared out front of the hospital tent for helicopters. Rachel hoped they didn't have anyone hurt *that* badly.

They hopped back in Scott's truck and rode up to the blast site. Several security guards stepped forward along their drive, but just waved them on when they realized who was driving. A couple gave Rachel knowing grins that she didn't want to think too much about.

I'm the source of rumor and conversation among the miners? Eek. It took them almost five minutes to make the trip, thanks to all the men walking along the road and the steady stream of emergency vehicles coming and going along the dirt mining road, which really wasn't anything more than a narrow flat strip of mountain carved out almost wide enough for two vehicles to pass side by side, but not quite. As they pulled up to the edge of the blast site, a security guard did step up to the truck's window.

"Mr. Morrison, you'll have to leave the truck here. We've got a parking area cleared off over to the right, but it's emergency vehicles only past this point."

"No problem, Stanley," Scott replied, and pulled the truck into a flattened graveled area. The three teens clambered out, and Scott looked them over.

"Stick close to me. We're not technically supposed to be allowed up here, but I think we'll be fine as long as we keep our heads down," he said.

"You know, we have been here before, Morrison. I've been coming to this mine since I was a little kid." Billy stuck his jaw out and crossed his arms.

"Sure, Billy. But what does your dad do anytime something goes wrong up here? Sticks you at home and goes off to take care of it. Well that's what they'd do today, too, except we're not going to let them. So, come on, I'd like to make sure my dad is okay and then get the hell out of here before whatever that thing was that cooked Mr. Stephenson comes back for another snack."

Rachel looked up at the clear sky, then followed quickly along behind the boys. Her dad was sitting on a rock near the edge of the crater with an EMT kneeling in front of him. Ben Hampton's pants and shirt were torn or scorched, one hand was wrapped in gauze and medical tape, and his shoes were gone, but he looked mostly unharmed. His brown hair, usually pulled back in a neat ponytail, hung loose around his soot-smeared face, but Rachel couldn't see any blood from where she was.

"Dad!" she yelled, running down the slope to her father.

He stood and caught her in his arms, then stuck out a hand for balance to keep them both from tumbling down into the center of the crater. He hugged Rachel tight to his chest, then put both hands on her shoulders and held her away to look at her face.

"What are you doing here? Why aren't you in school?" he asked.

"They dismissed any of us with parents up here. It's not like we were going to get anything done for worrying, anyway. So, I came to see if you're alright. I was so worried, Dad. I saw that video and that, that *thing…*it could have killed you! Oh my God…" She trailed off and buried her face in Ben's chest, suddenly sobbing uncontrollably. Ben turned stiffly and helped her sit on the rock. He waved the EMT away and held his daughter while she pulled herself together.

"I'm sorry, I'm silly, I know." Rachel sniffed, then took the handkerchief that Scott offered. *Oh my God! Scott! Oh crap, he just watched me fall apart like a little kid. Can I just die now?* Rachel's internal monologue ran like a bullet train as she blew her nose and dried her eyes. She tucked Scott's hanky into her jeans pocket and murmured a quiet "thank you" to him.

"Don't mention it," Scott said, then turned his attention to her dad. "Mr. Hampton, what was that thing?"

"What thing do you mean, Scott? We had a little accident with the blasting, but I don't know about a *thing*."

"Mr. Hampton, you've heard of cell phone cameras, right?" Scott said with a little half-smile on his lips. "Well, Cindy Jones is Mike Jones' little sister. And Mike is one of the security guys on first shift up here. Well, Mike has a new phone that he's pretty proud of, so he shot a little video of your whole topping this morning, and he didn't stop taping when things went bad. Mike sent it to Cindy, and you know how that goes. I'd be willing to bet that the first fire truck hadn't even gotten here before half the school had that video on their phones. So what was that you were saying?"

Ben sat down on the side of the slope and put his head in his hands. "Fuck. That's going to be a problem."

"Rachel, your dad has a gift for understatement. Scoot over," Scott said, taking a seat next to Rachel on the rock. "Now what was that thing?"

"I have no idea," Ben said, not looking up. "I've never seen anything like it."

"Really?" Billy said, looking around at everyone. "Is nobody going to say it? 'Cause I will, if none of you have the stones. That, my friends, was a mother-lovin' dragon."

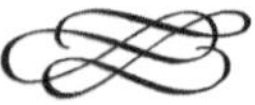

CHAPTER 4

"There's no such thing as dragons, Billy," Ben said, putting on his best "talk to young people" voice.

"Really?" Billy raised an eyebrow. "So what would you call something with big-ass wings, a long tail, a scaly body, long neck, and a shitload of teeth that just happens to come up out of the ground and, oh yeah, *breathe frickin' fire?* What would you call that if not a dragon?"

They stood in silence for a moment before Rachel spoke. "Well, it's sure not a Chihuahua. So whatever it is, we need to figure out where it went and what it's going to do when it gets there."

"I hope you don't have a mouse in your pocket, missy, because there is no 'we' in this equation. What *we* need to do is go home, put enough aloe on our burned feet to lube up a slip n' slide, and let the authorities deal with this. What *you* need to do is drive your poor wounded father home, help him into the La-Z-Boy and wait on him hand and foot, literally, for the next several days," Ben said, struggling to stand, wincing as he put weight on his scorched feet.

He turned to Scott. "What *you* need to do is find your father. He talks all the time about how much of a help you're turning into around here. Well, this is the time to step up and prove him right. He needs to be surrounded by people he can trust right now. The authorities and upper management will be looking for someone to blame, and if your dad isn't careful, he's going to find himself elected."

"And you," Ben said to Billy. "I don't even know what the hell you're doing here in the first place, but it better consist of helping Rachel get me into the car and then getting your ass home."

Billy opened his mouth to protest, but Ben held up a finger. "Unless you want me to call your dad and ask him what the hell you're doing here."

"No, sir. I'd rather that not happen," Billy replied, finding great interest in his shoelaces right at that moment.

"Fine, then. Get in the car." Ben waved at his Ford Escape hybrid, parked near the ambulances. The EMT gave him a hand getting into the passenger seat, and he handed his keys to Rachel. She slid behind the wheel as Billy hopped in the back seat. Scott came over, and Rachel rolled down her window.

"So, I'll get your bike taken care of bring it by your house later?" he said, making the last a question. "Maybe we could get some pizza and hang out?"

"Sure, that would be cool. Do you like games? I just got a new expansion to *Pandemic*, and I'm totally addicted. Billy can come over, and we can all three have board game night."

Scott got a look on his face like he'd just drank sour milk, but he choked out a smile and said, "Sure. That would be awesome. I'll see you guys over there about seven? That should give me plenty of time to get all this handled and get your wheel straightened up."

He stepped back and Rachel started to roll up the window. "I'll see you tonight," she said.

Scott gave her a little wave and stepped back from the car. Rachel turned the SUV around and started slowly making her way down the mountain to the base of the mine. Her head was in a whirl, but she didn't know whether to shout about it or faint. Scott Morrison was coming over to her house! What did you wear for that? She couldn't ask Billy. He was sitting in the back seat not speaking and acting all weird. She sped the car up, trying to get home quickly to call her best girlfriend, Cindy. Then she remembered that Cindy's mom was a first shift mine employee, and that snapped her focus back to the morning's events.

"Dad, how many people were hurt? Was everyone killed?"

"No, sweetheart. I think there were only four people killed, when all was said and done. Ed, of course, he was the first. Then a pair of guards I didn't know real well, then Ricky from the PR department. He tried to go up and talk to the thing after it was breathing fire."

"Isn't that what you did?" Rachel accused.

"What? No! That's not at all what I did! I tried to talk to it before it hurt anybody, and I probably could have kept things calm if that jackass hadn't tried to shoot the…whatever it was. Then there was all that fire, and I just tried to get down and stay out of the way."

"Good move," Billy chimed in from the back seat.

"So, Dad, when you were talking to the dragon, what language was it speaking? We couldn't make it out on the video."

"We couldn't figure it out either. It's not Chinese, Hindu, Arabic, or any other dialect we recognize."

"But you're sure it was trying to communicate?" Billy asked.

"Yes. I'm sure. It didn't attack until it was fired upon, but when it retaliated, it did so with extreme prejudice," Ben said.

"And now the government is coming to hunt it down and kill it." Rachel was surprised at how conflicted she felt about that. On the one hand, it had killed nice old Mr. Stephenson. On the other hand, it was a *dragon*! It really didn't get much cooler than that. Part of it was like living in a fantasy novel, only not the fun parts with the magic and the quests, but more like the parts where a vicious dragon ate the nameless characters before the hero got to town. That had all gotten way more real than she wanted.

Rachel dropped Billy off at his house and headed home. She didn't bother mentioning coming over to hang out with Scott, deciding that it probably wasn't a great idea with the way he was acting.

Ten minutes later, she turned off the main road onto their winding gravel driveway. Their house was a white two-story colonial farmhouse set more than a quarter mile off the road. She parked the SUV on the front lawn right by the steps and walked around to open the passenger door. Her dad stepped out onto the grass and grimaced. Rachel quickly slid his arm over her shoulders and helped Ben limp up the steps onto the porch into the front room of the house.

She settled him onto the IKEA sofa they'd brought with them when they moved to West Virginia and helped him put his feet up on an ottoman that, like most of their furniture, had seen better days. It wasn't that they were poor, or even that her dad didn't know how to keep house. It was more that neither of them really cared a lot about what the place looked like, as long as it was clean and comfortable. Of course, today Rachel was keenly aware of every scratch in the coffee table as she thought about Scott Morrison coming to visit.

"Is there anything I can get for you?" she asked her dad, sitting in the matching beige armchair.

"I'm good," Ben replied, then gasped as he shifted his feet on the pillow. "Maybe a couple of Advil would help."

"I'll get them." Rachel stood and headed for the kitchen. She dug through the medicine drawer and found the pill bottle. She poured her father a glass of ice water and carried the glass and pills into the living room. Her father was already asleep, his right arm bent behind his head and his left hand dangling off the couch beside him. Rachel smiled down at him and grabbed a light gray throw blanket off the back of her armchair. She unfolded the throw and draped it over her dad's chest and legs, careful not to touch his injured feet. She settled into the armchair with her battered copy of *Mistborn* and read for a couple hours until it started to get dark. Rachel looked over at her father and saw his chest rising and falling in a slow, relaxed rhythm.

Guess I'm on my own for dinner, Rachel thought as she went back toward the kitchen. She made a quick turkey sandwich, put it onto a paper plate, sprinkled a few chips beside it, and sat down at the kitchen counter with her book to eat. An hour later, she was long since finished with her food and totally immersed in her book, elbows on the counter and mind in another world entirely.

Her attention snapped back to this world as she heard the crunch of gravel in the drive. She looked out the window and recognized

Scott's truck pulling up beside her dad's SUV. She stepped out the screen door just as Scott lifted her bike out of the back of the truck and started walking toward the porch.

"Hey," he said. He stopped at the bottom step and looked up at her, holding the bike on one shoulder. He'd changed since she last saw him at the mine. He looked good—strong legs poking out of khaki cargo shorts, sneakers, and a navy blue West Virginia Mountaineers hoodie completing his high school boy uniform.

"Hey, yourself." She walked down the steps to meet him. *Nice legs,* she thought, giving him a long look as she got close.

"I brought your bike. It didn't take them any time to get your wheel back in true."

"I figured it wouldn't be too bad. I wasn't going that fast when I wrecked." She took the bike off his shoulder and carried it up onto the porch. She knelt and pulled the lock out of her bike bag and started to fasten the bike to the porch railing.

"Are you really worried about somebody coming out of the woods and stealing your bike?" Scott said, looking around at the acres and acres of nothing surrounding the farmhouse.

Rachel blushed and concentrated on her bike lock. "It's a habit, I guess. We lived in Atlanta before we moved here, and if you didn't lock your stuff up there, there was no chance of ever seeing it again. I guess I just haven't gotten over that mindset yet."

"Yeah, I can totally understand that. I mean, you've only lived here for what, three years now?" Scott sat on the top step next to where Rachel knelt.

She scooted over onto the step beside him and slugged him in the shoulder. "Shut up. Just because you own the town doesn't mean new people can't move in."

"Oh they can, but they have to meet certain standards of intelligence and attractiveness. You passed, by the way." Scott laughed.

"Like there was ever a question. When the competition in town is dogs like Jessica, a beauty queen like me has nothing to worry about," Rachel said sarcastically.

"Jessica's not bad, I guess."

"Not bad? Like I'm supposed to believe you weren't totally checking her out this morning when you almost killed me!" Rachel slugged him again, but this time, he caught her wrist and held her arm.

Scott looked deep into her eyes. "Why you hitting on me, Hampton?"

"I'm hitting you, Morrison, not hitting *on* you. There's an important word you're forgetting, rich boy."

His eyes flashed dark, and he let her go. "Sorry. My mistake." He stared out across the front yard for a long moment, then stood. "I gotta go. See you tomorrow."

"Wait!" Rachel cried, a little more sharply than she'd intended. She grabbed his hand and pulled him back down to the steps. "I'm sorry. I was just playing around. I didn't mean anything by it."

Scott shook his head and gave her a rueful half-smile. "Nah, it was me. I'm sorry. I just get a little sensitive about the whole rich kid thing sometimes. With people like Billy around, it's hard to know who means it and who's just playing around."

"Well, I was just playing around, and I mean that." She smiled at him, and Scott smiled back. They passed a couple of hours just talking about school, music, movies, and everything but dragons and mines and rich parents. Rachel realized with a start that she had talked more to Scott in one night than she'd talked to most kids in her class in three years.

The sun had set, but there was plenty of moonlight to see by in the early fall evening. Rachel shivered, and Scott pulled her close. "You cold?"

"Not now. I have this big warm boy holding me, so I'm all toasty."

"Good. I like my women like I like my coffee —"

"Hot and black?" Rachel grinned.

"Well, hot at least." He smiled down at her, and then their lips touched. Rachel felt a heat growing in her chest as they kissed, then her lips parted and her tongue tasted his mouth. Scott's arms tightened around her, and she tilted her head back, giving herself completely to the kiss.

And then the front door slammed and the porch light flicked on. Rachel pulled back, looking around. Her father leaned in the doorway behind the screen door looking down at them. "Hello, Scott. I see game night was cancelled. Or was it?"

"Hi, Mr. Hampton. How are your feet feeling?" Scott scrambled to his feet to stand in front of Rachel's father. He put his hand out, but Ben just looked at it. After the silence built to an uncomfortable level, Scott pulled his hand back and put both hands in his back pockets.

"I'm fine. How are you two? Keeping warm out here? I'd hate for either of you to catch anything," Ben said, giving his daughter a level look.

"We're fine," Rachel answered breezily, completely ignoring her father's sarcasm. "You feel better? You were snoozing pretty good there for a while."

"Yeah, I guess I really needed the nap. But I'm awake now, and you should be doing homework. Or dishes. Or cleaning your room. Or something."

"I get the hint, Dad. Scott, I've gotta head inside." She stood up, and the three of them stood in an awkward triangle looking at each other for a long moment.

Scott finally broke the silence and stuck out his hand. "I'll see you around, Mr. Hampton." Ben shook his hand this time, and Rachel could tell by Scott's wince that her dad had put a little extra something in the handshake.

She stepped forward for a hug and maybe a goodbye kiss, but Scott stepped backward so fast he almost fell off the porch. "I'll see you at school tomorrow, Rachel."

"Yeah," she said, examining the tips of her shoes. "I'll see you there."

Scott looked up at Ben's expression and blanched. "Yeah, I'll see you tomorrow. At school. Where we go. Together. To school, that is. Um, bye." He turned and almost ran to his truck, jamming it in gear and turning around to head home like he thought someone might chase him if he drove too slow.

Rachel stepped up to her father and looked him in the collarbone. At 5' 4", she couldn't look him in the eye when they were both standing, but she was so angry she felt like she'd grown a foot in the last five minutes. "It's a good thing you were attacked by a dragon today," she hissed. "Or I would absolutely kick your ass right now." She put a finger across her father's lips as he opened his mouth to speak.

"I love you, and I respect you, and I'm sure we will have this fight in the morning. But right now, I am going to go to my room and rant and rave and call you unspeakable things while assaulting Mr. Perkins and asking him why I have the most ridiculous father in the free world. I realize that it's immature and unreasonable to behave like that, so I'm warning you now that I'll be doing all of those things, so you should probably just leave me alone until the sun is up and you can apologize properly. Preferably with bacon." Then she pushed past her father and stormed into the house.

She managed a pretty good storming, she thought, as she stomped up the stairs. She slammed the screen door pretty well, then slammed the front door so hard the glass rattled, but didn't break anything. Then she clomped up the stairs like an angry elephant, stood at the door to her room for a count of three, then slammed that door hard enough to make a picture fall off the wall across the hall from the bathroom.

Once safely in her room, she grabbed her stuffed penguin Mr. Perkins and flopped down on her back in the middle of her bed, a grin splitting her face from ear to ear. "He kissed me, Mr. Perkins. A real kiss, with lips and teeth and tongue, even!" She hugged the pudgy penguin tight to her chest, rolled over, and went to sleep without even kicking off her shoes.

CHAPTER 5

The moon was high when Auros woke, and he was cold and dirty. He disentangled himself from the deer carcass and stood, walking out into the clearing. He looked up at the sky, the moon and stars shining down upon his naked form. He smiled up at the moon, a familiar friend from so many years ago, but when he looked at the stars, he frowned.

That doesn't look right. The stars are not in their proper places. How long have I slumbered? How long since men took over this world and forced the dragons underground? And where are the elves? Why have they not awakened us? Do they still hide among the men?

He shook his head, long golden hair flowing around his shoulders. Auros looked down at his human form and smiled. It was a pleasing form, but not his true body. He concentrated, and the air rippled around him in a shimmering golden light. His human body glowed, then seemed to expand within the light until a huge winged dragon stood in the clearing.

Much better, Auros thought. *But also much hungrier.* He snaked his neck through the trees back to where he had left the deer carcass and quickly seared the meat with a blast of fire. He used his snout and fangs to flip the deer over and seared the other side, burning off the thin layer of forest dirt the body had picked up in the hours it had lain there.

Auros dragged the deer into the clearing and using his razor-sharp fangs and his foreclaws ripped the deer to shreds. He ate the meat almost raw, savoring the blood as it dripped down his elongated chin. When he had devoured most of the deer, he dug a small hole with one rear leg and pushed the remains into it. After all, only a true beast leaves its kill just lying around to smell and draw scavengers.

Then the dragon pointed its snout to the sky and used its magic to float lazily above the clump of pine trees surrounding what he had already come to regard as his clearing. Once above the tree line, Auros stretched out to his full wingspan, well over forty feet from tip to tip, and flapped mightily. With his enormous wings flapping and a glowing nimbus of magic surrounding him, Auros flew, slowly at first, then faster and faster into the night sky.

Feeling grimy from his years of slumber and more than a little bloody from his meal, Auros flew east looking for a lake large enough to submerge himself. One more sign that he had slept for many hundreds of years—there were men here. Not just the nature-loving men who had hunted these hills before his slumber, but many men. Pale, soft men with strange carriages and tubes that fired thorns or stones that tore at wings. The shape change had healed his hurts, but Auros tried to avoid the gathering places of men as he flew, not wanting any more injuries at the hands of these puny creatures.

Finally, he spotted a lake with nothing surrounding it but trees. A small lake, but plenty deep enough for him to submerge his entire body, it had none of the caves or huts of men nearby. Auros tucked his wings in tight to his body and dove into the clear blue water, letting the silt and grime of ages wash from his scales. He emerged with an enormous splash into the night sky, casting a silhouette across the landscape that had not been seen over this continent in many hundreds of years.

After several rounds of diving and flying, diving and flying, Auros settled into the water, using his powerful hind legs to paddle along the surface of the lake. His wings spread out just under the water, keeping his head and forelegs afloat. The dragon rested like that for several hours, just floating and lazily scrubbing his scales clean with the tops of pine saplings that he plucked from the ground like ten-foot tooth-picks. Eventually he had restored the gleam to his hide and refreshed himself in the cool mountain water, and he saw the beginnings of the sunrise peeking over the mountaintops. *I should go. I would not enjoy it if men found me here and forced me to slay them. I must make them understand me somehow. Perhaps I can mind-speak to one of them?*

The dragon dove under the surface and swam rapidly from one end of the lake to the other, building up speed as he went. As he approached the shallows on the far end of the lake, he burst into the air, using his magic and his mighty wings to hurtle skyward, spraying a huge jet of water across the nearby trees and sending one startled squirrel tumbling from his nest to chatter angrily at the dragon from the ground. Auros chuckled to himself as he flew, a low rumbling laugh that started deep in his belly and bubbled up to finally break free into a sound of pure joy at his newfound freedom, his restored beauty, and a sheer love of flight. All too soon, he was back at his clearing, tucking his wings to his sides and shifting into his human form as he touched ground. He walked slowly through the woods for a time, listening with his mind as much as his ears, until he heard an unfamiliar sound approaching.

There was a whirring sound and a crunch of leaves and twigs as if by footsteps, but the tread was too rapid and too heavy for anything he'd ever heard. It was a consistent thrashing through the underbrush and along the narrow trails through what he had already begun to think of as his wood, and he went to investigate. He heard the strange humming sound approach and stepped out in front of the intruder, determined to see what was making such a bizarre sound. He realized too late that it was a human, a girl human on some strange kind of two-wheeled pony, and she was rushing blindly through the forest with little concern for anything around her. She looked up as Auros stepped onto the path, and her eyes widened as she realized a collision was inevitable.

She swerved her metal pony off the path and crashed hard into a mighty pine tree, hurtling over the front wheel of her steed and landing motionless in the underbrush. This quest to save the humans was not getting off to a very good start at all.

CHAPTER 6

Rachel woke before her alarm and groaned. She stretched out across her bed and thought back to the previous day. *Definitely one of the strangest days in history.* First, she wrecks her bike, then she makes a date with Scott Morrison, then there's a dragon attack at the mine, then Scott comes over to her house and he kisses her! Then her dad's a big asshole and runs him off. No wonder she passed out still dressed. But now she was *really* uncomfortable. Her belt and shorts were tangled all around her, her bra was cutting into the underside of her boobs, and her shoes had left muck all over the bedspread, which was her problem, since she did all the laundry. *Bleh. Might as well get up and get a shower. It's almost time for my alarm anyway.*

She stood, stripped to her panties and t-shirt, and stumbled to the bathroom. Her dad was coming out of his bedroom, ready to go to the mine. "You still mad at me, punkin'?"

"Give me time. Right now I'm still asleep. So you've got a little grace period. How are the feet?"

"Sore, but the aloe helped a lot. I can't wear my work boots, so I'll have to stay in the trailers up at the site entrance today. No investigating the explosion for me."

"You mean the dragon's lair."

"We're not talking about a dragon. Dragons don't exist." Her dad slid past her in the hallway on his way downstairs. "You want breakfast?"

"Pop-Tarts?"

"Fine." He sighed and limped down the stairs. Rachel watched him go, paying attention to how gingerly he was walking. He was hurting a lot more than he wanted her to know. *Silly men, always trying to hide things from us,* she thought as she went to the bathroom for her morning ritual.

A little less than an hour later, she was sitting at the table looking a lot like a girl who'd spent exactly no time considering her outfit, hair, or makeup. In reality, she'd washed her face and reapplied her makeup twice and gone through five different rock band or comic book t-shirts before finally settling on a vintage Sunnydale Razorbacks shirt from *Buffy the Vampire Slayer.* She was halfway through her second Pop-Tart when her dad set down his coffee cup and cleared his throat. *Here it comes.*

"I want to talk to you about Scott Morrison," Ben began.

"Nothing to talk about. I think he's cute and nice. I want to go out with him. He wants to go out with me. Case closed."

"Oh no, case not closed. Case not even close to closed, young lady. Gerald Morrison is my boss, and Scott is his oldest son and heir apparent. I cannot have you chasing after him and making me look bad. It could make things difficult for me at work, and I don't have enough seniority here to let that slide. Not to mention what would happen if the two of you got serious and then broke up. I'm sorry, sweetheart, but this is a good job, and I can't have you doing anything to jeopardize that." He picked up his coffee cup and pretended to sip, but kept his eyes on Rachel's face, waiting for the inevitable explosion.

He got it. "Tough. Look, Dad, I went along with moving here because you said this was a good place and an awesome opportunity for you. Before that it was New Mexico. And before that it was Texas. So I'm a little tired of us moving from crappy town to crappy town for your job, and doing everything in the world to keep some asshat boss of yours happy. I've got a life here too, now. I'm *sixteen*, and apparently not hideous to look at, so I'm going to date. And I'm going to date boys, no matter how much you dislike the idea. And the boy in question right now is Scott Morrison. He's the best thing going around here right now—smart, rich, and above all, *nice*. I'm not talking about marriage. I just want to go out with him, have a little harmless fun."

"That fun didn't look so harmless last night on the porch." Her father put down the coffee cup and crossed his arms across his chest.

"Oh my God, we were just kissing! He didn't even touch me! And I didn't touch him!" *Ummm, but I wouldn't mind running my fingers across that broad chest.* Rachel shook herself and got back to the argument at hand. "Dad, did you miss the whole 'sixteen' bit? I've never even French-kissed a boy before last night! I'm so much a virgin I'm practically a nun! But I like Scott, and I am not going to stop seeing him just because you're scared his dad won't approve of him going out with a geologist's daughter."

"That's not it at all, sweetheart. I just don't want to see you get hurt."

"Well, I will! It's going to happen, so why not get it out of the way early? I mean, look, it's not like your track record of relationships is anything to write home about…" She saw as soon as she said it that she'd gone too far. The vein in her dad's forehead popped out a little, and she could see the muscle in his jaw clench. "Dad, I'm sorry—"

"Don't be. You're right. I haven't dated much since your mother *abandoned us*. Because I didn't want you to get hurt again. I didn't want you to get attached to someone and then have her walk out. Again. But my dating record isn't the point here. The point is, you're my daughter and you are sixteen years old and you will do as you're told. And I'm telling you to stay the hell away from Scott Morrison." He stood up from the table very slowly and walked to the sink. He put his coffee cup down and limped out of the kitchen, down the short hallway to the front door, and out onto the porch. Rachel could hear him clump down the stairs, get into his SUV, and drive off.

She sat there for a few minutes cursing herself for her stupidity, then ran her fingers through her hair, pulled it back into a loose ponytail, and stood up herself. She put her plate and glass in the sink, gave the dirty dishes there a silent promise to take care of them after school, and went out the front door, locking it behind her. She knelt by her bike and started to unlock the chain, and then the tears came. *It's so unfair! I don't want to drink, I don't do drugs, I don't even know if I want to sleep with Scott, but I know I like him. And he acts like he likes me. And he's fun to be around and sooooo pretty. Why can't Dad see that?*

Her thoughts whirled around her head like a cloud of bumblebees as she put her bike on the trail behind her house that led to the school. Most days she stuck to the roads, but today she felt like being a little reckless, and ripping through the trees as top speed seemed like just the thing. So she pushed off hard and pointed the bike toward the trees, wiping the tears off her cheeks with the back of her hand.

Seconds later, all her concentration was absorbed in not running headlong into a tree. The three-mile ride was barely enough to break a sweat most days, but she was riding a lot harder than usual. After the first mile, Rachel slacked up her pace just a little and slowed down to enjoy the ride. The sun-dappled forest was still damp with dew, and the violets in the undergrowth hadn't ducked away from the morning sun yet. It was going to be a warm day, but there were still enough patches of deep shadow to raise chill bumps, and the faintest hint of honeysuckle brought a smile to her face as she remembered another reason she liked West Virginia so much more than Texas or New Mexico. *It's so green here, even in winter.*

She let her mind float away to thoughts of a certain junior boy with the moonlight playing through his hair as she rode the familiar trail. There were only a few tricky parts to this ride, and they were at the beginning and the end of the trail, most of this middle bit was just a nice ride through the peaceful woods, with nothing more dangerous than a confused squirrel or startled rabbit running in front of her wheels.

What the hell is that? Holy shit, that's a boy! A naked boy in the middle of the woods! Rachel's thoughts ran wild as Auros stepped out from behind a tree directly in front of her. He was a vision of chiseled hunkiness, bare-assed naked in the woods, with long blond hair falling over his shoulders, a jawline that belonged in a Captain America comic book, and Chippendale-worthy abs. *And oh my goodness...*

Her thoughts flashed white, then black as she smashed hard into a tree and flew off headfirst into the underbrush.

~

Rachel's head hurt. A lot. She didn't open her eyes for a minute, just lay still trying to figure out exactly how many places hurt and wiggling her fingers and toes to make sure she still had feeling in all her extremities. She did, but several of those extremities had pretty painful feelings in them. And she was getting cold lying in the damp grass and moss. After a few seconds of mentally going over her checklist to make sure everything still worked, she tried to sit up.

And couldn't. She made the effort, but as soon as she started to rise, there was a weight across her chest that held her down. She finally opened her eyes and started as she looked into the gold-flecked green eyes of the most beautiful boy she'd ever seen. He sat beside her, leaning over her with one arm pressing her into the moss-covered ground. *That's why I can't get up. I am trapped by a hunk. Good reason.* She tried again, and he pushed her back down, shaking his head.

"I'm going to sit up. And you're going to get over it. I don't know you, and I sure don't know why you're running around naked in the woods, but that's your deal. I have to get to school, though. And now I need to go home and change clothes. So while I normally don't mind being ravished by blond hunks in the woods just after breakfast, today's not a good day for me." She tried to rise again, and still he kept her pinned. The hunk reached over with his other hand and touched her left temple.

"Ow!" Rachel jerked away as his touch flared bright pain in her head. He let go of her chest to take her head in both hands. He closed his eyes and put his forehead to hers. *Definitely creepy. Why are all the really pretty ones always psycho? It's like a law or something. Hey, what?!??*

The pain in her head disappeared, and a warm sensation rushed through her entire body. It was a little uncomfortable, like her body temperature had suddenly risen five degrees. Of course, that might be caused by the naked hottie leaning over her and pressing *all* the way against her body. She shifted a little, trying to get a little space between her legs and his really, really warm flesh, but he threw a leg over hers and held her tight.

This is definitely more than I'm comfortable with on a first date. Rachel struggled a little, but the hunk just tightened his grip on her head, and that flush rolled through her again, starting in her toes and going all the way to the tips of her ears, lingering in several places that were injured in the fall, and a few more interesting places that didn't hurt, but now throbbed a little uncomfortably. After a few more seconds, Goldilocks, as she'd come to think of him, let go of her head and moved back to sit cross-legged facing her.

Wow, this one's the opposite of shy. Rachel sat up and scooted back, putting a little distance between herself and her rescuer, who also happened to be the cause of the accident, so he didn't get full brownie points for the rescue.

"Who are you? And what the holy hell are you doing butt-naked in the middle of the woods at seven-thirty in the morning?" Goldilocks just sat there, looking confused. He closed his eyes, held his hand forward, and Rachel felt a *shift* in her head. She reeled, blinked rapidly, and when she opened her eyes, it was like a weird case of double vision. She was looking at Goldilocks, but she was also seeing herself. It was like she was looking through her eyes and his all at the same time.

"What the hell was that?" She tried to scramble to her feet, but the weird vision thing was screwing with her balance, and she sat back down with a thud.

My name is Auros, not Goldilocks. It is a pleasure to meet you.

"Who said that?" Rachel craned her neck to look behind her, trying to find the source of the words. She hadn't seen Goldilocks' lips move, so it couldn't have been him.

She saw him smile out of the corner of her eye and whirled back to him. "Do you have a buddy out here? Is that your game? You kidnap high school girls and have your way with them? Well, I'm not an easy target, asshole!" She once again tried to stand, but still couldn't quite figure out where to put her feet. After several long seconds, she managed to gain her footing and put her back to a towering oak.

I am alone. I do not understand your speech. What is a high school girl?

"This is not going to work. I don't know how you're throwing your voice, but quit it!"

I have blended our awarenesses so that I may speak with you. I mean you no harm, and there will be no lasting effects. I give you my word.

"Well, that would mean something if I had any idea who you are. But since I don't, your word isn't worth crap to me. Now get out of my head and let me go to school!" She shook her head, trying to evict her unwanted passenger, but all she accomplished was a wicked case of vertigo. The forest started spinning, and she sat down again to keep from revisiting her Pop-Tarts.

Foolish girl! You understand nothing of me, and you question my word? Has your world changed so much that men are all liars now? Is there no trust? I am an honorable...man, and have but limited need of you. Once we are finished here, you will be free to go.

Rachel could feel the depth of the insult she had laid on Goldilocks. Her questioning his honor was one of the nastiest things she could have said to him. She might as well have said he mated with lizards, whatever that had to do with anything. And what did he mean about needing her? She had a few thoughts about how she wouldn't mind being needed, but...

Rachel saw Goldilocks blush, and her own cheeks flamed. *He heard that!*

I heard that, he replied inside her head.

You really are inside my head?

I really am inside your mind. For a brief time. I do not understand your speech, and I must learn it quickly. This is the most expeditious method.

Well, if you've already moved on to words like "expeditious" then I think you're pretty far along.

I am considered a quick learner among my...people.

That's a blessing, I suppose. I do still have to get to school, and I can't exactly ride with you hitchhiking my vision like this. Oh shit! My bike! Not again. Rachel stood on wobbly legs and held an arm out to the boy.

"Help me get over to my bike." She pointed at the frame lying beside the tree. Auros took her arm and helped her over to her bike. She righted the mountain bike, then flipped it over to rest on the handlebars and seat, wheels in the air. She knelt by the pedals and turned them slowly, checking the wheels. The spokes all looked okay; the front wheel seemed to still be true. She stood up, flipped the bike over, and checked the brakes and shifters. Everything looked fine, except the handlebars were a little off center. She reached under the seat, got out her bike tool, and made a quick adjustment to the hex screw in the center of the bar. A few twists later, and everything was good as new.

The same could not be said for her helmet, which had suffered the same fate at the one she had worn the day before. It hit the trunk of the pine tree and split right down the middle, transferring all her kinetic energy into the helmet and saving her from a concussion, or worse. But that meant that now her *spare* helmet was toast, and she didn't have another. *Oh well, I guess I'm living dangerously until I can make it to the bike shop after school. I keep going like this and I should buy stock in bicycle helmets.*

She gathered up her backpack, a few pens that had flown out of it, her iPhone, which had miraculously survived the crash, and her lunch bag. Then she stopped, shook her head, and looked back over at Goldilocks. "You're not in my head anymore."

"No, I am not," he said, smiling. "I have absorbed enough knowledge to speak with you, so now I no longer need to invade your thoughts."

"Oh. Good." *Not like he's not going to be in my thoughts for a loooong time. Mrow!* "Well, I'm Rachel." She stepped forward and stuck out her hand.

"My name is Auros."

"And now you're dressed." She just realized that he was wearing jeans, Converse sneakers, and a plain green t-shirt. "Where did your clothes come from?"

"I conjured them. I saw that my nakedness made you uncomfortable, so I dressed. Do people always wear clothes now?"

"Yes, always. Whenever we're going to be around other people, we wear clothes. Where are you from, dude?"

"That, I believe, is what you would call a long story. And you mentioned having to go to school?"

"Yeah, I've got to get to school." She found herself filled with a strange feeling as she said that, a longing of some sort, like she really wanted to see this strange man again. And not just for the obvious reasons. "Will you be here when I get done? Can I see you again?"

"I would like that. I have much to learn about men now. I hope you will not mind teaching me."

"Well, I wouldn't say I know much about men…" She grinned what she hoped was a saucy grin, then faltered at the blank expression on Auros' face. *You idiot, he means mankind!*

Rachel blushed again, making what had to be a record number for her in a twenty-four-hour period, and she mumbled, "Yeah, I'll teach you anything you need to know." Her face flamed even deeper crimson as she listened to herself, and she picked up her bike and pointed it toward the school.

"I will be here when you return," Auros said, holding one hand up.

"Yeah, um, see you later." Rachel still didn't look at him as she rode away, face on fire.

If there's anything in the world to make the school day seem longer than meeting a hot naked boy in the woods first thing in the morning, Rachel couldn't figure it out. And, of course, she couldn't tell anybody about it. It's not exactly the kind of thing you bring up in geometry, after all. *Guess what, Sandy? I almost got myself concussed to death when I took a header off my bike because a naked stud was loitering in the woods behind my house this morning!* Yeah, she could just see having that conversation with any of the girls in her class, not that she had much in the way of conversations with them on most days. And talking to Billy about it was out of the question, with as nuts as he'd gone over her just talking with Scott yesterday.

Oh crap, Scott. Then there was Scott. Last night she was making out with him on her porch like he was the last boy on Earth, and for a little while at least, she really thought he *was* the only boy on Earth, and then here comes Goldilocks—sorry, Auros—in all his naked glory, and she's completely forgotten about Scott.

I'm a slut. A terrible person. A complete tramp. But he was sooo pretty. He had muscles in places I didn't even know there were places, and that golden-bronze skin...yummmm. Rachel shook her head, trying to focus on the biology lesson, but the mating habits of praying mantises just couldn't keep up with the movie in her head.

Finally, the day was over, and Rachel headed to her bike, wondering if Auros would really still be there. *Did he really wait for me all day in the woods? With nothing to entertain himself? No TV, no Xbox, not even a book? Or did I imagine the whole thing?*

"Hey Rachel, wait up!" A voice snapped her out of her reverie, and she looked around. *Oh shit.* Scott was jogging to catch up to her, a dazzling grin across his face. He held a shopping bag with *Bike World* written on the side. He caught up to her and held out the bag.

"I forgot to give you this last night. I felt really bad when I saw you ride in this morning without a helmet." She opened the bag and pulled out a box.

Her eyes went wide when she saw the helmet. "Scott, this is too much! I can't take this. This is like a hundred-twenty-dollar helmet!" She was holding a Giro helmet in black and purple. It was a sleek, top of the line mountain bike helmet, much better quality than the crappy Walmart helmet she'd cracked up. It was a very expensive gift, especially given the way she was going through helmets this week.

"The guy at the store said it was the best. So, I got it. And I'm not taking it back, so you might as well put it on." Scott smiled.

"Yeah, it's a great helmet." Rachel hesitated for another moment, then tore into the packaging and quickly adjusted the helmet to fit her head. It was a sleek helmet, designed for maximum speed while still protecting the head from impact. The top and sides were heavily vented to keep the head cool, and it had a detachable sun visor on the front for open-air rides. She put it on, and it felt almost like she wasn't wearing a helmet, it was so lightweight.

"Wow, Scott. This is awesome. Thank you *so* much!" She threw her arms around his neck and hugged him tightly. Scott hugged her back, then held on as she started to pull away. He looked down into her eyes and leaned forward. Rachel closed her eyes and tilted her head up, opening her lips slightly as their mouths pressed together. The world disappeared as they kissed, only to come rushing back at the whistles and catcalls from other students heading out the front doors of the school to their cars and bikes.

They pulled apart, and Rachel felt her cheeks flame *again. This is nuts! I don't blush. Except around Scott. Or Auros. Okay, I only blush around pretty boys that kiss me, or naked boys that scare the shit out of me in the woods.*

"What are you doing this weekend?" Scott asked.

Rachel's head snapped up as she remembered the guy waiting for her in the woods. "N-nothing," she stammered. "Why?"

"I was wondering, um, if you'd like..." Now Scott was the one stammering and looking at his shoes.

Rachel decided to end his suffering. "Yes. I'd like. Now what would I like?"

Scott looked up from his sneakers to the sparkle of Rachel's green eyes. "I dunno. I hadn't gotten that far yet. Can I think on it tonight and pick you up tomorrow around ten?"

"It's a date. I mean, it's not a date. I mean, is it a date?" She looked up and got lost for a minute in his smile, mocking but at the same time totally not making fun of her.

"Yeah, it's a date, but it won't be a big thing. Wear jeans, or shorts, or something you don't mind getting dirty. Or maybe wet."

"That doesn't help, Scott. So far all you've managed to rule out is prom dresses."

"Yeah, definitely don't wear a prom dress. Well, not tomorrow, anyway. We'll get to that later." He grinned.

She grinned back at him. "Oh, we will? Prom's like three whole months away, mister. Don't you think you're counting your chickens before they're hatched?"

"Nah. I think I'm counting on you liking me at least three months' worth." He grinned at her again, leaned down and kissed her quickly on the lips, then turned and headed off toward his truck. "See you tomorrow!" he called over his shoulder.

"See you," Rachel murmured, running a finger across her lips where the warmth of his skin still lingered. She shook herself out of her daze and unlocked her bike from the rack, walking it to the head of the trail behind the school. *Oh crap, Auros!* she thought as she swung one leg over her bike and headed into the woods. *A couple of days ago I didn't have any boys interested in me, and now I've got two. That is, if Auros is really interested. I mean, maybe he is, maybe he isn't. Oh crap....*

Rachel's head was still awhirl when she rode into the clearing where she'd left Auros. He was sitting cross-legged on the ground, dressed this time, and rose gracefully as she braked in front of him.

"That was a much more comfortable way to stop, I believe, than this morning." He smiled at her.

She grinned back. "Yeah, it's a whole lot easier on the head and neck, too. How was your day? What did you do all day, sit here and talk to the earthworms?"

"No, I do not speak the language of the earthworms. I did, however, learn to converse with the sparrows, and I learned a great deal from them. I also hunted and fed. Would you like some deer?" He pointed over to the remains of a deer lying on a bed of moss a few feet away. One haunch was completely gone, and the rest of the body looked burned somehow, but Rachel saw no evidence of a cooking fire.

She tried to hide her disgust at the animal lying dead in front of her, but failed miserably. She did manage to keep her lunch down, though, which she considered no small victory. "No thanks, I had lunch at school."

"So be it. And how was school? And for that matter, what is school?" Auros sat back down and motioned to the ground beside him.

Rachel sat nearby, leaning against a tree. "What do you mean, what is school? Where are you from?"

"That is, as I said, a very long story, and I am not sure you would believe me if I told you. For now, can we agree that I am from some-where very different from this place and proceed as if I understand nothing, which may be nearer to the truth than you know?"

"Sure. I'll pretend you just dropped down out of a spaceship from the planet Nebulon and this is your Earth school before I take you to my leader." She paused. "You're not really from outer space, are you?"

"I don't know what that is. I am actually from very near to this place."

Hillbillies. Some of them might want to think about coming down the mountain more often than when the still needs fixin'. Rachel started talking, and talking, and talking. Auros seemed to know absolutely nothing about the world, but whenever she pressed him on it, he got all mysterious and refused to explain. Finally, as the sun started to set, she realized that her father would be home soon, so she stood to leave.

"Will you be okay? Do you need anything? I've gotta go, but I could maybe come visit you tomorrow." She remembered her date with Scott and smacked herself on the forehead. "No, wait! I can't come tomorrow, but maybe the next day? Can I come see you Sunday?"

"What is Sunday?" the strange boy asked.

"Oh jeez. We didn't go over the days of the week. I didn't think I needed to. Apparently, I was wrong. Today is Friday. Tomorrow is Saturday. The day after that is Sunday. I can't come see you tomorrow, but I can come back on Sunday. Is that cool?"

"That is acceptable to me. Does that mean cool?"

"Close enough. You know, for a guy who's only a little older than me, you use some weird dialogue."

"I am much older than I appear. Goodbye. I will await you on Sunday."

Rachel hopped on her bike and took the trail home, riding at an easy pace while her mind raced along at a thousand miles an hour. She had a date tomorrow with Scott Morrison! But Auros was soooo cute. Weird, though. He said he was from around here but didn't even know the days of the week? That was über-weird. And she hadn't seen Billy all day. She hoped he wasn't mad at her for hanging out with Scott. She knew Billy kinda crushed on her whenever he wasn't with someone, but she'd never felt anything for him but friendship. He was more like her brother than a friend. She just hoped he wasn't too upset by what was going on with Scott because he really had a bug up his ass about the Morrisons.

She was still lost in thought when she pulled up into her yard but snapped out of her fog when she saw an unfamiliar vehicle in the driveway. It screamed "Federal Government" as loud as if there had been a carnival barker riding atop the black Suburban with black tinted windows. She gave it a quick once-over, noting the black rims, the way it sat really low on its tires, like it was even heavier than a normal Suburban, and became instantly suspicious. She'd seen government pukes come out to mines her dad was working in the past, but none of them had been rolling this kind of wheels. Usually it was some pencil-neck in a white pickup with the Bureau of Land Management or Environmental Protection Agency logo on the door, but never an armored SUV with blacked out windows.

Her dad's Ford Escape was nowhere in sight, and there was a man in a suit sitting on their front porch steps. He had his elbows on his knees and his pants rode up just enough for Rachel to see his expensive black Ecco loafers. This dude hadn't been to the mine and had no intention of going there. Not in three hundred dollar shoes and a tailored suit. He stood up and waited as she walked toward to the porch.

"Miss Hampton." He stepped forward and extended a hand. Rachel nodded at him and put her bike helmet in his outstretched hand.

"Thanks," she said, sliding past him and locking her bike to the porch rail. She finished, stood up, and retrieved her helmet. She put her helmet and backpack down by the door and leaned on the porch railing. There was no way in hell she was inviting this dude into her house with her father gone. He looked harmless, but something about him *felt* wrong. Like he was out of place in his skin, or something.

It wasn't a bad-looking skin, either. He looked young for a government guy, maybe thirty, about six foot, a little under two hundred pounds, with broad shoulders and a trim waist that the cut of his suit emphasized. *It's a good thing the 80s didn't really comeback into style. The last thing this dude needs is shoulder pads!* He had long blond hair pulled back into a slick ponytail and cheekbones so sharp Rachel thought they looked almost unreal, like an artist's rendition of the perfect human face, right down to the Roman nose. His only concession to being kept waiting on the porch was to loosen his tie a little and undo the top button of his dress shirt. *Or maybe he does that to make himself look like he's defying authority, like he's bucking the dress code. Get the teenager on your side by showing how cool you are.*

"You lock your bike up all the way out here?" He smiled as he asked.

"We've had some unwanted visitors." Rachel kept her voice neutral, not sure why she didn't trust the man. He didn't seem to notice.

"Well, please, allow me to introduce myself. I'm Ted Bentley, from the government. We're here to help." He stood and handed her a card. Rachel stuck it in her back pocket without looking at it.

"You're here about the dragon, right?"

"Well, we understand that something anomalous was discovered during the excavation yesterday, and we have been dispatched to assist local authorities in learning exactly what that anomaly was."

"It was a dragon." Rachel was enjoying the man's discomfort now and decided to push his buttons just for fun. "You know, big, wings, breathes fire—dragon. It left."

"And how do you know it was a dragon and not some type of mass hallucination?"

"Because mass hallucinations don't make for good YouTube videos. And that's how I saw your anomaly. So why don't we cut the crap and you tell me who you really are, who you really work for, and what you really want, and maybe I'll tell you what I saw."

"I can't do that, Miss Hampton. It's a matter of national security. I'm sure you understand."

"Then I can't talk to you anymore. It's a matter of my personal security. I'm sure *you* understand and will remove yourself from our property immediately." Rachel opened the door and set her backpack and helmet in the house. "Goodbye, Mr. Bentley. Good luck catching your anomaly."

"Thank you, Miss Hampton. I'm sure we'll be seeing each other again soon." Preston walked down the steps and started across the yard to his Suburban. "If you think of any helpful information, please call the number on the card."

"Oh, I certainly will." Rachel closed the door and threw the deadbolt, then went upstairs to her room, where she watched the Suburban disappear down her long driveway in a cloud of dust.

CHAPTER 8

Ted Bentley allowed himself a little smile as he drove away from the Hampton house. He reached into the center console of his Suburban and put a Bluetooth headset into his left ear. He pressed the button and said, "Dial office."

A few seconds later, a pleasant recorded female voice answered. Before the auto-attendant could even begin her spiel, Bentley said, "It's Bentley. I have news. Connect me."

The connection was made almost instantly, and a low baritone voice came on the line. "Bentley. What do you have for me?" The voice glided over his ears like liquid gold, warm, inviting him to unfold all his deepest secrets. Bentley was unaffected. It had been many years since such compulsions worked on him.

"She's been near the dragon. And recently. I could smell it on her. It wasn't strong, so the dragon may be in another form, but she's definitely seen it," Bentley said.

"Does she know?" the voice asked.

"I don't know, sir. I doubt it. When I asked her about the mine incident, she didn't seem to know anything about the dragon's shape-changing abilities. It's possible the beast has kept its true nature from her."

"How do you plan to find the dragon?"

"I planted listening devices throughout her home, and I was able to slip a tracker into her bicycle helmet. The reports we have are that she rides everywhere, so we should be able to follow her. With any luck, she will lead us right to the dragon."

"Luck?" the voice asked. "*Luck?* This is the moment I have waited centuries for, Bentley, and you wish to trust it to luck? Are you a fool, or simply the world's greatest optimist? There is no luck besides that which we make ourselves. Follow this girl. Do not let her out of your sight. If she goes near the dragon again, I want you right behind her. And if it's shifted, then it will be all the easier to capture. Do not fail me, Bentley. Not now, when we are so close."

"No, sir. I won't." Bentley pulled off to the side of the road to get control of his shaking hands. He had never heard his leader so determined, so focused.

"The age of men is almost over, Bentley. This dragon is the last piece of my puzzle. Once we have it, we have the world. Again. I will await your call telling me that you have the dragon." There was a sharp *beep* as the connection was severed.

"Yes, sir," Bentley said to an empty line. He put his head against the steering wheel of his Suburban and took several deep breaths before putting the SUV back into gear and heading into town. The girl would lead them to the dragon eventually, and perhaps his commander would give him his own continent to rule. Maybe Australia. He'd always wanted to see Australia.

CHAPTER 9

Saturday morning dawned sunny and warm. Rachel flew out of bed and bounded down the stairs in her normal weekend house clothes, a tank top and tattered gym shorts. She turned the corner into the kitchen at a fast skip, only to freeze in the doorway as Scott Morrison looked up at her from her kitchen table. Scott and her father sat at the table sharing the newspaper and a pot of coffee. Rachel's mind locked as she saw the sun glint off Scott's hair in the eastern sunlight, and she almost fell into the kitchen, drawing both men's gaze.

"Good morning, sweetheart. Scott was just telling me what he had planned for you two today." Her father grinned at her. "Would you like some toast?"

I hope to God he didn't tell my father everything he has planned, or I'm going to die. Unless he doesn't have anything planned, in which case I'm going to die for completely different reasons. "Um…no, I'll just grab a Pop-Tart. Hi, Scott! You're here early." She felt her face stretch into a tight grin that she hoped didn't make her look too psychotic. "I…um…just need to grab a quick shower, and I'll be ready to go." She turned to run back up the stairs, arms crossed against her braless chest.

"No need for all that. You'll probably get wet before the day's through anyway." Rachel whirled back to Scott, eyes wide. "We're going fishing, Rachel. Surprise!"

Surprise, indeed. No wonder her dad had that stupid grin on his face. He knew how horribly her last fishing trip had gone, with the worms and the scales and the stink. It's not like she was a girly-girl, but worms icked her out in a huge way. This wasn't exactly the romantic picnic in the woods she'd been hoping for, but that explained her dad suddenly treating Scott like he was a favorite nephew. *Traitor.*

"Well, uh…just let me throw on a swimsuit in case I decide to jump in after those fish." She gave Scott her best smile, then caught her dad's eye and gave him the kind of evil look that only daughters can properly deliver. Rachel turned and ran back upstairs, trying desperately to come up with some way to salvage her date. Inspiration hit her as soon as she pulled out her swimsuit. Living hundreds of miles from any ocean, she only had two—a utilitarian one-piece she wore to swim laps at the school pool and a skimpy two-piece she wore to lay out in her back yard. She put on the two-piece, then brushed her hair into a quick ponytail. She pulled on a pair of flip-flops, some cut-off jean shorts that stopped just about an inch below the bikini bottoms, and another tank top, this one an old one of her dad's, so washed and tattered as to reveal more than it hid.

Rachel looked around her dresser, then saw what she was looking for behind her hairspray. She grabbed the scissors and chopped off the bottom half of her tank top revealing her flat, tanned stomach. A quick spritz of deodorant and a little dab of perfume in all the important spots, and she was back down the stairs. No need to give her father too many opportunities to murder her date, after all.

Conversation screeched to a halt when Rachel stepped into the kitchen this time. The pretty teen looked like something out of a music video, just trashy enough to be fun, without crossing any lines her father could say anything about. She caught sight of the purple sheen spreading from his neck to his ears and threw her arms around his neck.

"I'll see you tonight, Daddy. We'll be back around nine or ten."

Then she kissed him on the cheek and whispered, "And that's what you get for not warning me he was here."

Rachel took Scott's hand and led him out the front door, pausing to grab a Pop-Tart and a Coke on the way out. She skipped down the steps and out to Scott's truck, which now had a silver and black fishing boat on a trailer behind it.

"I hope you know how to drive that thing," she said. "Because I don't know the first thing about boats."

"Don't worry, Rache. I've got this covered," Scott said, opening the passenger door for her. He walked around the truck and double-checked the hitch before getting into the driver's seat and putting it into gear.

The longest part of the trip was getting out of her driveway. Once they navigated the windy gravel road, it was a matter of minutes to get to the lake. Scott backed the boat down the landing and told Rachel what to do to make sure the boat didn't float away as he parked the truck. She sat behind the controls, looking around at all the knobs, levers, and gauges until Scott came back carrying a cooler.

"Lunch," he declared, heaving the cooler over the side. "I almost forgot it." He grinned up at Rachel from where he stood waist-deep in the water. "Give me a hand up." He reached up with his right hand, and Rachel leaned over. He gave a tug, and she tumbled face-first into the water on top of him!

Rachel came up spluttering and soaked to the skin, blowing water from her nose and mouth. She looked at the grinning Scott, who had jumped into the boat without any need for assistance, and narrowed her eyes. "You'll pay for that, mister. I don't know how, and I don't know when, but you will most certainly pay for that."

Scott grinned and reached down, helping her into the boat. "But now you don't have to worry about getting all wet today. You're already soaked."

"You're right, thank you so much!" Rachel leaped at him, wrapping her arms tightly around his chest and soaking him through. She clung to him, making sure that his t-shirt was completely drenched before pulling away.

"Nice. Oh well, won't need this anymore, then." Scott laughed and pulled his shirt over his head. He grabbed a beat-up baseball cap from the floor of the boat and jammed it on his head. "You're gonna want a hat, too. Did you bring anything?"

"Sorry, left my bonnet at home," Rachel replied.

"I keep a couple of spares in the storage compartment under the seats with the life vests. Grab a couple of vests and a hat, and we'll get going."

"Life vests? I can swim," Rachel protested.

"Not if you hit your head on something. No vest, no boat. It's my dad's rule, and it's a pretty good one."

Scott obviously wasn't going to move the boat until she put on a vest, so Rachel decided to torture him a little in the process. She went to the locker on the back of the boat, bending from the waist to open it. When she was sure she had Scott's attention, she pulled out a pair of life vests and tossed one to him. Then she stood in front of him and peeled off her sopping wet tank top, leaving her in only her turquoise bikini top. She gave Scott a big smile, then put the bulky orange life vest on over her head, covering much more of her than the tank top ever had. She pulled a yellow West Virginia Mountaineers baseball cap on, threading her ponytail through the hole in the back, and sat down again.

Scott muttered something she couldn't hear and turned around to crank the boat.

"What was that?" she asked.

"Nothing."

"No really, what did you say?"

"I said I wasn't sure what was going to kill me first, your dad or your teasing." Rachel laughed as the boat started off, heading for Scott's favorite "fishing hole," whatever that meant.

The lake wound around the base of several mountains, with plenty of open water for skiing and swimming, but several secluded areas as well, little inlets created by the local geography. They pulled into one of these a few minutes later, pushing through some low-hanging branches to turn into a still cove that was almost completely hidden from the rest of the lake. Rachel shivered a little bit in the shade, and maybe a little bit more in anticipation of spending time with Scott in this romantic haven, but her shivers turned to frustration when he pulled out a pair of fishing rods and started to bait the hooks.

"You're really going to fish?" she asked. She looked down at herself. Even in the stupid vest, she looked pretty cute. She had nice legs. She'd even made time to shave them this morning after her humiliation at the breakfast table. She noticed that Scott had taken his vest off when he set the anchor, so she followed suit, enjoying the feel of his gaze on her body.

"Well, yeah. That's kinda the point of the day, isn't it?" He handed her a rod and turned back to his tackle box. "I baited the hook for you. Your dad said you didn't like bugs."

"Thanks," Rachel said, flicking her wrist and casting her line into the water. *Note to self—patricide now an option.*

Scott moved back to the bench seat next to her and put the bait bucket between their feet. He tossed his line out and watched the bobber contentedly. "This is the life," he said. "Beautiful day, beautiful girl, no worries. Perfect."

"Beautiful?" Rachel murmured. She looked down at herself again. She was a lot of things, but beautiful never made the list. She was okay, nice body, maybe a size or two too big for *Elle* or any of those stupid magazines, but decent enough. She had nice hair and not much in the way of zits, but beautiful?

"You really think I'm…beautiful?" she asked, her voice quivering a little as she looked up at Scott's jawline. The dappled reflection of the sunlight played across his brow, making the flecks in his eyes sparkle and his brown curls seem alive.

"Well, yeah, Rachel. Have you ever looked at yourself? You're a knockout. You're one of the prettiest girls in school. Totally beautiful."

"So beautiful I've had three dates in three years here. Counting today."

"Well, I hope you count today. I went to all the trouble to cook. Well, not really, but I did drive through Bojangle's and get a box of chicken for lunch." He gave her that lopsided grin again, and suddenly it seemed very warm in their shady little cove.

"Hey! You've got a bite!" Scott leaned forward and patted her thigh. She turned to look at the bobber, which was going, going, and now completely submerged.

"What do I do?" Rachel asked, flailing around trying to grab the pole.

"First you get the pole," Scott said, trying unsuccessfully not to laugh at the frantic girl.

"Okay, now what?" Rachel grabbed the pole and held it out from her body like a poisonous snake. She gave Scott her best "helpless girl" look, and he slid over behind her, wrapping both arms around her to grab the fishing pole with his hands on top of hers. In this position, Rachel couldn't help but feel his strong arms around her, and his muscular chest pressed into her nearly bare back. As an added bonus, from his angle, Scott couldn't see the knowing smile on her face as she snuggled into his arms.

Scott gave the rod a yank to set the hook and said into her ear, "Okay, he's on the hook, now reel him in."

Just what I was thinking, Rachel thought. She reeled the fish in slowly, making sure not to lose contact with Scott's bare chest at any point. Eventually, she reeled the fish in, then turned in Scott's arm and jumped up and down a little, not enough to rock the boat danger-ously, but enough that he knew she was there. She also managed to *thwack* him in the side of the head with the fish, a wriggling little crappy about eight inches in length. *That's what you get for dunking me, smartass.*

"Hey!"

"Sorry!" She gave him her best "innocent look," big kitten eyes and everything, and he just shook his head.

"Damn, you're cute, but not much of a fisherman." He reached for the fish, expertly pulled it from the hook, and threaded it onto a stringer in a bucket of water he kept sitting in the bottom of the boat. "There. You've got the first fish of the day."

"So, we're done? Now we get on to the laying out in the sun part of our program?"

"Not even close, missy. How are we going to make dinner out of just one fish? I plan to be hungrier than that. Watch my rod while I bait your hook again." He moved away, a little reluctantly Rachel thought, and put a cricket on her hook.

She squirmed a little at that for real and averted her eyes. It wasn't that she loved crickets in particular, but jabbing a fishhook through something just seemed so harsh. Oh well, it didn't hurt to let Scott feel manly once in a while. He certainly felt manly pressed up against her back. Rachel's face flamed, and she bent over, ostensibly reaching for a bottle of water, but hiding her face for a few seconds, too.

They fished most of the morning away, and by the time Scott was willing to call a lunch break, Rachel was starving and more than a little sweaty. Finally, when their stringer was loaded down with more crappies than she thought anyone would ever want to eat, Scott pulled up the anchor and cranked the engine again.

"Lunchtime?" Rachel asked hopefully.

"Lunchtime. Just a few minutes, though. I've got another favorite spot I'd like to show you, if you can hold off for a little while longer."

"Sure, I'm just wasting away here. No worries."

"Grab a banana out of the cooler. We'll have lunch in fifteen minutes, I promise. And we're not going far. I won't even make you put the vest back on." Rachel thought that might be as much for his benefit as hers, but she didn't mind.

CHAPTER 10

He steered the boat out of the cove and down the shoreline. After about five minutes, he turned into another inlet that Rachel hadn't even noticed until they were right on top of it. It was almost completely hidden from the rest of the lake, but when they turned in, Rachel's mouth dropped. Tucked away from the rest of the lake was a fifty-foot circular lagoon with a raft floating in the dead center of it.

"Welcome to my hiding spot. The fish never bite here, but it's a great spot to get away and chill. The mining company owns all the shoreline on this part of the lake, so we don't have to worry about anybody building a house to spoil the scenery, and I've never run into another person all the time I've been coming."

"How did the raft get here?" Rachel asked.

Scott pulled the boat up to the fifteen-foot square raft and cut the motor. He tied off and stepped over the side. "I towed it in, then I sunk five-gallon buckets full of cement from each corner. They're attached to the raft with big eyebolts, and I buried the end of the chains in the cement before I pitched them over. The raft only moves about five feet in any direction. If you want a quick dip before we eat, go ahead. The water's plenty deep. I dive off this thing all the time." He was obviously proud of the raft, and Rachel didn't begrudge him that. It was pretty cool, and well-built. All the boards were sanded, and the thing looked solid as a rock.

Rachel stepped out of the boat onto the raft and took a running start across the planks, knifing into the water with barely a splash. She swam underwater for a long minute, then popped up almost all the way over to the shore. She turned back and saw Scott standing on the raft, mouth hanging open.

"I told you I could swim," she called, laughing.

"Yeah, but you didn't say you were half-dolphin! Is eating what we caught this morning going to feel like cannibalism?"

"First off, dolphins aren't fish. Secondly, at this point I'd almost eat *you*, I'm so hungry..." She realized how her words might be taken and she blushed again. *Dammit! Just once today I'd like to open my mouth and find something there besides my foot. Shit! There I go again.* She dove under the water and swam the rest of the way back to the raft. She pulled herself out of the water easily and stretched out on the wooden platform to dry for a minute before diving into the spread Scott was preparing.

"Soup's on," Scott called just minutes later.

Rachel rolled over and her eyes widened at the spread before her. In addition to the promised Bojangle's fried chicken and sweet tea, Scott had mashed potatoes, mac-and-cheese, and what looked a lot like homemade peach cobbler. "Wow. Scott, this looks amazing. Did all this come out of that little cooler?"

He chuckled. "Yeah, well, kinda." He leaned into the boat, and she saw an insulated picnic basket that had lived under one of the seats until now. "The cooler was just for ice and the tea. Dig in."

She did. Rachel dove into the chicken and sides with what her dad would have called a "decidedly unladylike appetite," but she couldn't care less. She was *hungry*.

"So where did you learn to swim like that? I thought you used to live in Texas," Scott asked a few minutes later.

Rachel had a mouthful of spicy chicken and held up a finger in the universal signal for "my mouth is full, gimme a second."

After a few seconds of frantic chewing and a couple of mouthfuls of sweet tea, she was able to answer. "Not just Texas, but Texas *then* Arizona. But we had pools at our apartment complexes, and there was no better place to spend all summer than at the pool."

"Torturing boys with that bikini?" Scott grinned.

"Nope. This one is just for torturing you, pal." She chunked a piece of ice at him and laughed.

He ducked and threw a handful of cubes from the cooler. "Well, it's doing its job. You've been driving me nuts all morning." He leaned closer, and his lips brushed hers. They kissed lightly, then Rachel reached up behind his head and pulled him in tight. Her lips parted, and their kiss deepened. They sat there for a long moment exploring each other's mouths before Rachel pulled back.

"That's a lot of fun, and trust me when I say I really want to keep kissing you…" she said, dropping her eyes.

"But…" Scott said.

"But I'm starving, and if you start kissing me, I'm never going to get any food!" They both laughed and sat back, concentrating on their food for the next few minutes. Before long, the two teens were left with the decimated remains of a box of chicken and sides, and the half gallon of sweet tea was nothing but a memory.

Rachel started to clean up the mess, but Scott waved his hand at her. "No way, chica. This is my shindig. The guests do not do the cleaning up." He got up and started gathering boxes and Styrofoam containers.

"I am a liberated woman of the twenty-first century, and if I want to help clean up my mess, I will." She stuck her tongue out at him and kept cleaning. It was the matter of just a couple of minutes to gather their trash back into the picnic basket and stretch out on the raft with a couple of bottles of water.

"Now what?" Rachel asked. *Not that I don't like lying here in the sun with a beautiful boy lying next to me.*

"Well, we really shouldn't go back in the water for at least half an hour after eating," Scott said.

"And I'm kinda fished out for one day," Rachel replied.

"Hmmm...what shall we do?" Scott asked, rolling over onto one elbow.

"Gee, I don't know," Rachel said, kissing him lightly on the nose. "What shall we do?" She pulled him down and kissed him, wrapping her arms around his neck.

Scott rolled over onto her, pressing his muscular torso to her damp skin. He kissed her lips, then moved down to her chin, planting a trail of kisses along her jawline to her ear, where he nibbled softly, then moved down the side of her neck, kissing all the way to the junction of her neck and shoulder.

Rachel's hands played over the muscles of his back, tracing his spine with her fingernails. She dragged her fingertips along the edge of his shoulder blades, running her hands through his hair as his kisses left little pools of liquid fire on her chin, her ear, her neck. His movements became more frantic, his hands playing across her stomach, reaching upward to cup her breast, his thumb moving under her bikini top to the tender flesh there. She felt the heat spread throughout her body and started to see sparkles behind her closed eyelids, then suddenly realized where they were, what they were doing, and who she was doing it with. She froze, unable to move, and Scott pulled back.

"Hey, are you okay?" he asked. His breath was coming in short gasps, like he'd just run a race.

"Uh...fine, but I think...uh, we need to slow down a little." Rachel sat up, scooting backward on her butt to put a little more space between them.

"Sure, no problem." She could see the disappointment in his eyes, and it mirrored what she felt in herself, but she *couldn't* go any further. She'd already let him touch her where no other boy had touched her.

"I'm sorry, I didn't mean to lead you on. It's just, I'm..."

"Hey, it's cool. Seriously. I'm cool. I wasn't expecting anything out of today but a little fishing and a nice picnic with a pretty girl. Mission accomplished. Anything else is up to you, I swear." He grinned at her, and Rachel felt a little better.

"I'm sorry. I really like kissing you, but I don't want to move too fast…"

"Rachel." He leaned forward and took both her hands in his. "I'm cool with going as slow or as fast as you like. I'm not in a hurry. It's not like we're going anywhere. I'm just a junior. We've got the rest of this year and all of next year before I need to think about going anywhere. So there's no hurry. Really."

"All next year? The rest of this year?" Her head whirled at what he was saying. "You're talking like we're dating."

"Aren't we?" He looked away, like her words hurt him somehow.

"I…I don't know. I'd like to. But…it's not like we *know* each other…"

"Rachel, I didn't propose marriage. I just want to go out with you. And I want to go out with you more than once. So that makes us, by definition, 'dating.' So what if we don't know each other, that's what dating is for, right? Getting to know one another?"

She smiled. "Yeah, I guess. But I have to ask, if we're 'dating,' does this mean you're not going out with anyone else?"

"No. I mean, yes. I mean, I'm only interested in dating you. I've wanted to ask you out for months, ever since I first saw you up at the mine one Saturday with your dad, walking around like you owned the place, completely fearless."

"Oh my god, I was being such a tomboy!" She covered her face with her hands.

"No! I liked it. I love the mine. I love the raw natural power of the place, and I like that you aren't scared of it, like so many girls are. It's one of the things I first found attractive."

"What else do you find attractive?" She gave him a shy smile and scooted forward, wanting to be close to him again.

"Your hair, your beautiful, wild, crazy hair that does whatever it wants." He reached across the gulf between them and took a curl between his fingers. "Your lips, the way they light up the room when you smile." He brushed the curl across her mouth, bringing a giggle out of her. He scooted closer, and Rachel matched his movements with her own. They both leaned in, and his lips met hers again. She tasted the slight sheen of sweat on his lip, then his lips parted and their tongues danced, twisting, probing, touching. She pulled back, slowly, reluctantly, teasing just a little. Rachel looked deep into his eyes and saw the hunger there, but there was something else. There was a patience there, a peace that she hadn't seen in the few guys she'd gone out with before Scott. They were always in a hurry to move on to the next thing, to see how far she'd let them go.

But one look in Scott's eyes and she could see he was different. He wanted her, she was sure of that. And she wanted him, she was *damn* sure of that. But not yet. Not here, and not yet. And she could tell by the look on his face that he was okay with that. Really okay with it, not just the kind of pretend okay with it that teenage boys affect when they want something but know they can't have it.

"You wanna swim some more?" he asked, his voice low and husky.

"No. I think I'm done for the day."

"Well, I think we've caught out limit, and we've had lunch, but I'm not quite ready to take you home yet." He flashed her another one of those relaxed grins that she was getting really used to seeing.

"Well then, I guess that means one thing—" she said.

"Sandbar!" they yelled in unison, and hopped up onto their feet. A quick look around the raft for any trash they missed and Rachel was back in the boat. Scott cast them off and hopped in himself, then fired up the trolling motor until they were safely off the raft. Then he cranked the big outboard motor and pushed the throttle all the way forward. The bow of the fishing boat rose up as they put on speed, and Rachel gripped the seat with both hands. She laughed as the small boat bounced across the still water, heading for the Sandbar in the center of the southern half of the lake.

The Sandbar started as just a little spit of dirt in the lake, but it grew over the years as boatload after boatload of high school kids brought buckets full of sand out to build it up. Nobody remembered how the tradition started, but every year before the first home football game, every player on the team brought a bucket of sand out to dump onto the Sandbar. It had turned into a huge tradition, one Thursday night every August when the whole town got together in fishing boats, pontoon boats, even a few old jon boats rowed out into the lake to watch as the players dumped a bucket of sand onto the bar for good luck.

Over the years, the Sandbar had become *the* spot to be on spring and summer weekends, even into early fall. Since its humble beginnings, the little outcropping of dirt had grown into a tiny island almost the length of a football field and half as wide. Some kids had built a firepit in the center, so now the first party barge every weekend was on firewood duty.

Rachel had been out to the Sandbar before with Billy and some other friends, but it wasn't where she usually spent her Saturdays. For one thing, she didn't have a boat or any plans of getting one. For another, she didn't have too much in common with most of the girls there. But this Saturday was different. This Saturday she'd show up in Scott Morrison's boat, her boyfriend's boat.

"Hey Scott," she called over the roar of the engine.

Scott throttled the boat down and turned back to her. "Yeah?"

"Are you my boyfriend now?" She blushed at the question, but she wanted to be perfectly clear where she stood with the boy, especially before she got cornered at the Sandbar by somebody like Jessica Baker. Or worse, Billy.

"Do you want me to be?"

"Why do you always answer a question with a question?" she asked, half-seriously.

"Just call me Socrates." He pronounced it So-crates, like the guy off the *Andy Griffith Show*.

"Okay, So-crates, will you be my boyfriend?"

"Do I get to kiss you some more?"

"Depends on the answer." She grinned at him. The sunlight reflecting off the water made sparkles dance in his eyes, or maybe that was just her imagination.

"Well, yes, I would like to be your boyfriend."

"Then you get to kiss me as much as you want. Unless my dad is around." She frowned, remembering her fight with her father from the morning before. "Then you might want to restrain yourself."

"I'd rather restrain you." He leered at her and waggled his eyebrows in his best imitation of a pervert.

Rachel laughed and stood up, walking to him at the controls. "Just wanted to clear that up. We can go to the Sandbar now."

"Not until I get my kiss," he said. "I was promised kisses if I answered correctly."

"I guess you were, weren't you?" She threw her arms around him and kissed him vigorously. His hip hit the throttle, and the boat lurched into motion, throwing them both backward into the driver's seat. Rachel slid off onto the floor of the boat with a thump, and Scott flailed around for a few seconds trying to get control of the boat. By the time he had the boat back on course, they had gone a quarter-mile in the wrong direction and were both laughing uncontrollably.

"They say the key to a long-lasting relationship is being able to laugh together," Scott said when his breathing was once again under control.

"Then we should just call a preacher this afternoon because obviously we'll be together forever," Rachel said from the floor.

CHAPTER 11

Saturday afternoon activities at the Sandbar were in full swing when they pulled up. Someone had brought a volleyball and a net, and a vicious boys-against-girls game was in progress, with shirtless boys showing off for their bikini-clad opponents. A couple of boys Rachel recognized from her biology class were digging a pit and filling it with firewood, while half a dozen girls lounged on beach towels nearby, laughing and teasing each other as they worked on their tans.

Scott pulled his boat up and lashed off to a pontoon boat. Rachel recognized it as belonging to Jesse Ryan, a guy she knew a bit from freshman English. He and Scott seemed to be friendly, though, slapping hands and hugging in that weird one-armed hug that guys do. Jesse helped Rachel up out of the fishing boat onto his barge with a strong grip, then turned to a cooler.

"Hey, Rachel. Good to see you out here for a change. Brighten up the joint a little bit. You want a beer?"

"No, thanks. Do you have any water?"

"Yeah, no problem. Right out there." Jesse laughed and pointed at the lake. Rachel laughed with him, then flipped him the bird. Jesse laughed even louder, then tossed her a bottle of Aquafina from the cooler. She followed Scott across the string of boats tied together, finally stepping off the last one onto the sand.

Scott pulled a bag off his shoulder and reached inside, coming out with a beach towel and a bottle of sunscreen. He spread the towel out, dropping his shoes on two corners to hold it in place. Rachel did the same with her shoes, securing the bottom corners of the towel in place and peeling off her t-shirt and shorts. She smiled to herself when she noticed Scott watching her. *It's nice to be appreciated, even if it is just for my body.* She congratulated herself on her choice of bathing suits. The bikini left just the right amount to the imagination, at least in her opinion. Rachel was pretty sure she'd be grounded until she was fifty if her father ever saw the bathing suit in question.

Rachel sat on the towel with her legs stretched out in front of her, digging her toes into the sand and feeling the warm sun start to bake into her shoulders. "Hey, toss me that sunscreen," she said to Scott, who squirted a big dollop into his hand and then pitched the bottle to her. She squeezed the lotion out and started rubbing it into her legs, arms, and face. A shadow loomed over her for a second before she felt Scott settle onto the towel behind her. His strong hands felt good on her shoulders as he massaged the sunscreen into her neck and back.

"Lean forward. I don't want to miss your lower back," he almost whispered. Rachel felt a chill run across her as his breath tickled her ear, and she bent over, almost touching her head to her knees. She could hear Scott's sharp intake of breath and giggled. He rubbed her back for a lot longer than it took to apply the sunscreen, but she didn't mind. After a few minutes of languishing under his warm fingers, she sat up and flipped over onto her stomach.

"Do the backs of my legs?" She looked up at Scott, whose eyes had gone wide. He stuttered something, then scrambled up onto his knees and started rubbing the backs of her legs. She reached around once to slap a straying hand, but he was mostly well-behaved. When he was finished, she sat up and motioned for Scott to lay down. He obliged, and she took the opportunity to admire the well-muscled back that was laying in front of her.

Rachel felt a smile creep across her face as she held the bottle of sunscreen high above Scott's back, letting the cool liquid splatter across him without warming it in her hands first. He jerked up, but laughed as she pushed him back down on the towel. Rachel took her time rubbing the lotion into his tan skin, then moved down to his long, lean legs. Her fingers paused over a white line running up the back of one leg.

"What's this?" she asked.

"I had to have some surgeries when I was little. My legs were pretty jacked up, and I had a bunch of operations to fix them. There's a steel rod in that leg."

"Really? I didn't know."

"Yeah, it sucked. I had a really bad limp when I was a kid and couldn't do anything sports-wise. But I had the surgeries and got over it." He flipped over onto his back and grinned up at her. "Do my front?"

Rachel laughed and squirted more lotion onto his stomach. "I think you can reach that yourself, big boy." He flashed her his easy smile and rubbed the sunscreen into his hairless chest.

They sat, sipping water and talking about school for a while, but Rachel kept seeing his eyes flick over to the volleyball game. Finally, she pointed over to the net and said, "Go play. I brought my Kindle, so I can read. Go work off some of that testosterone."

"You sure? I don't want you to be bored." But his eyes never left the game. Rachel recognized Barry and Britt and Mike, some of Scott's best friends from school. They were all rotating in and out of the game.

"Go! If I can't keep myself occupied with a trashy romance novel and a half-dozen half-naked men jumping up and down in front of me, I should have my girl card taken away. Now let me do my girl-friendly duty and look cute while you get all sweaty and dirty." She smiled when he didn't correct her for her use of the word "girl-friend" and pulled her e-reader out of her bag. She flipped to her latest book, some goofy thing about nerdy vampire detectives, and flipped her sunglasses down over her eyes. The book was okay, but nothing to write home about. And certainly nothing compared to the sight of Scott Morrison scampering around the sand in his swim trunks.

Rachel woke with a start at a loud motor pulling up to the Sandbar. She hadn't even realized she was asleep, so she was a little groggy as she picked herself up off the towel and stretched. Her sleepiness vanished when she recognized the boat—it was J.C. Preston's pontoon boat. Billy's cousin had outfitted his "party barge" with everything a ridiculous country teenager could want for his weekend lake enjoyment. He had an AstroTurf roof with driving mats to hit golf balls off of, a slide to go from the rooftop driving range to the water, a bamboo tiki bar, a huge sound system, and more strings of multi-colored Christmas lights than a *National Lampoon's* movie. J.C. was driving, as usual, wearing nothing but a pair of flip-flops and a neon yellow speedo, which did nothing but draw attention to his stick-thin frame. But J.C. was all about attention.

And Billy was where he was every Saturday—being towed along behind his cousin's boat in an inner tube. Billy looked at least as ridiculous as J.C., sporting fins and a snorkel to go with his beer hat and bright pink swim trunks. J.C. pulled into the mass of lashed-together boats and tied off, flipping a switch behind his bar and blaring the latest pop hit across the lake.

"The party has arrived!" he yelled into a microphone. The teens on the Sandbar applauded and cheered. As ridiculous as he was, J.C. was always good for a laugh, and no party was complete until he showed up with the music. After focusing on J.C.'s arrival for a few seconds, everyone went back to what they were doing, except for Rachel, who decided her reading time was probably done.

She stood and strolled over to the volleyball game and sat next to Scott, who was taking a breather sitting on a log by the net. "You just abandoning me?" she said with an exaggerated pout.

"Nah, just didn't want to wake Sleeping Beauty."

"You know you're supposed to wake Sleeping Beauty with a kiss. Does that mean you don't want to kiss me?" She made her pout even bigger, and Scott laughed.

"I've wanted to kiss you for a long time." He pulled her close and pressed his lips to hers. Rachel closed her eyes and parted her lips, feeling his strong arms around her, his broad chest against her, the splash of ice-cold water running down her back!

They broke apart, spluttering as cold water streamed down their heads and across both of their chests and backs. A chorus of laughter greeted them as J.C. stood over the couple, grinning like he'd just won the lottery. "No making out on the dance floor, goobers! Get a boat!" Scott jumped up and halfheartedly chased J.C. around the island for a few minutes before returning to Rachel's side. He had just sat down when Mike called out to him.

"Hey, Morrison! Get in here!" Scott shook his head at Rachel, and she made a shooing motion at him. He jogged back to the volleyball game, and Mike sat out for a few minutes.

Rachel watched the game, which had morphed from a laid-back boys-versus-girls game to a competitive all-boys affair, except for Cassy Settler, the star of the high school girls' volleyball team, who had a better serve than any of the boys, despite her short stature. Scott was on a team with Britt, Cassy, and another boy she didn't know, while J.C. and Billy headed up the opposite foursome. The game went back and forth with nobody really keeping score, but Rachel noticed that Billy kept shooting dark glances at Scott when nobody was looking.

This has all the signs of something that's going to end badly, she thought after a particularly hard spike from Billy narrowly missed Scott's face, drawing a scowl from her date. Her thoughts proved true a few minutes later when the two got tangled up in the net on a volley and both of them crashed to the sand. Scott hopped to his feet first and extended a hand to Billy, who reached up to take it. Instead of standing, Billy pulled hard on Scott's hand and yanked the taller boy down, rolling him over and pummeling his chest and torso. Scott returned the punches as best he could, but he was so taken off guard by the attack that he couldn't get his footing and mostly just managed to cover his face and head.

Rachel was up and sprinting to the fight as soon as she realized what was happening. "Grab your idiot cousin!" she yelled to J.C. He just stood there, yelling randomly at the sky, and Rachel knew she was getting no help there. Billy had Scott pinned and was raining punches down on the bigger boy's arms and shoulders when Rachel got there, so she just lowered a shoulder and tackled Billy to the sand. He threw an elbow without even looking and caught her solidly in the temple. Rachel's vision flashed, and she slumped over onto her back, dizzy from the blow.

"Rache? Oh shit, Rachel!" Billy turned to her, only to meet Scott's fist with his face. Scott was on his feet, and he threw roundhouse after roundhouse at Billy, driving the smaller boy back from the fallen girl.

CHAPTER 12

The great dragon slept, the forest floor churned to a comfortable loam beneath his claws. The dappled sunlight danced across his golden scales, alternating hot and cold across his body. His head lay on a huge boulder in a pool of sunshine, glimmering like a giant golden ingot in the forest.

In the blink of an eye, Auros roared to full consciousness, a sudden pain in his head flaring to life and snapping him out of his nap. He whirled around his clearing, looking for the assailant, but saw nothing.

"Who dares assault The Gold?" he roared, his whip-like neck raising his head to the tops of the pine trees surrounding him. No one was there. He closed his eyes, willing the pain to subside, but it wouldn't. The pain lingered, a phantom hurt with no visible source. He shifted to human form, but still saw nothing.

The dragon's heart raced, his fear palpable. His head throbbed, and in his mind's eye, he saw humans, many humans. Two of the humans fought, but Auros cared little. Humans always fight; it means nothing to dragons. Then his head flared with agony again, and he looked on as the world spun, and he felt soft sand under his back. In his mind, he looked down and saw soft, skinny legs, saw curves, saw arms with no scales, no muscles, no hair. Then he understood.

The girl. When he healed her, he must have transferred a sliver of his essence to her, tying their minds together. And now she was in pain, in danger from these stupid human males. And what hurt the girl, hurt the dragon. Auros let out a roar and took to the skies, rushing to the rescue of a silly human girl.

CHAPTER 13

Rachel lay on her back in the sand, glaring up at the cloudless sky. "Goddammit, you two, cut it out!" she yelled, struggling to her feet. She started toward the two boys, but a pair of skinny arms wrapped around her waist and lifted her off the ground.

She spun around in the unfamiliar grip and found J.C. grinning at her. "Hey there, cutie," he said with a smile. "You really don't want to get in the middle of those two right now."

"You really want to let me go before I knee you in the balls so hard they pop out of your ears," Rachel hissed in his face. Just as she was about to make good on her threat, she heard a tremendous splash behind her and a cavalcade of screams from the kids on the Sandbar.

J.C.'s face went three shades of pale, and he dropped her on her butt to land with an *oof*. She turned around to see what he was so nervous about, and her heart sank as she caught sight of the golden dragon standing in the lake, and the giant wave rushing toward the shore.

Scott and Billy froze where they stood as the wave crested and soaked them to the waist. Jessica Baker fell off the roof of J.C.'s boat into the lake and splashed around screaming for a solid minute before she realized that she was in the shallows and stood up. All eyes were on the golden behemoth as a head the size of a doghouse stretched out between Scott and Billy. Rows and rows of razor-sharp teeth gleamed in the dragon's mouth, and its forked tongue flicked out like a snake's, as though it were tasting the air.

"Stop this foolishness. You have injured the girl-human. And you make my head hurt," Auros' voice boomed across the lake. All eyes turned to Rachel, sitting on her butt at J.C.'s feet.

"I'm not hurt. Really. But, um, thanks for worrying about me?" She reached up, and J.C. helped her to stand. Rachel walked to the edge of the Sandbar and stood eye to eye with the dragon. "Do I...know you?"

In answer, the dragon stood on his hind legs, reached out with a foreleg, and grabbed Rachel around the midsection, then unfurled his enormous wings and took to the sky. Rachel shrieked in terror as the giant claws closed around her, then screamed again as the ground fell rapidly away.

"Put me down!" she yelled as the lake shrank beneath her.

"I don't think you want me to do that." The dragon swiveled his head around on his long neck to look Rachel in the eye. "You would likely not survive the fall. I will put you down soon, and I will return you to the other humans safely. Do not fear."

"Do not fear? *Do not fear?* I'm flying a hundred feet above a lake in a dragon's claw and you're telling me not to fear? Are you insane?"

"I do not believe so. I have been asleep for a long time, but I do not believe I have lost my mind. And we have arrived." The dragon tipped his wings and flew in a tight spiral down into his clearing. He set Rachel down softly on a bed of moss, then summoned his magic. A golden glow surrounded him, softly at first, then brighter and brighter until Rachel had to look away. When she looked back, the blond boy she'd met in the woods a few days ago stood before her, clad in flip flops, yellow swim trunks, and nothing else.

"A-auros?" Rachel said, her eyes wide.

"Yes. I apologize for frightening you, but I felt it would be better not to approach again in my true form. I fear your world has forgotten much of dragons."

"Well, I think you just gave them a big reminder, pal." Rachel sat down on a moss-covered rock, curling her toes into the soft earth. It was cooler under the trees, and she felt a slight chill. She looked back at Auros, trying to reconcile the image in front of her with the enormous dragon that flew her to this secluded spot.

"Where are we?" she asked, looking around. "This isn't where I met you." After riding her bike through the woods near her house, she knew them like the back of her hand. She knew there weren't rocks like this out there. And was that a stream she was hearing?

"We are not far from that place. This is closer to the lake, yet far enough from the dwellings of men that I would not be seen flying to you."

"Yeah, what was that about, anyway?"

"I do not understand your question, I am sorry. I have slumbered for many years, and when last I conversed with men, you spoke the tongue of Elves or other civilized beings, not this crude language of your own creation."

"Fair enough, if a little condescending. Why did you come break up Billy and Scott? You said they made your head hurt. How?"

"That is my fault, I fear. There is a certain…transference of essence inherent in close magic. When I healed you, I seem to have formed a slight…bond, if you will."

"Like you can read my mind?" Rachel scooted back on the rock until her back was to a tree.

"Not exactly. I can feel extreme emotions, or when you are in pain. When you were injured, I felt the pain. I do not enjoy pain, so I sought to end the conflict before the children caused you further injury."

"Thanks. I think."

"I know this seems strange to you, Rachel. But I mean you no harm, and I will allow no harm to come to you. We are bonded now, you and I, and that tie cannot be easily severed."

Rachel looked at him, eyes brimming. Her heart raced with conflicting emotions. He *seemed* nice, and was really pretty, but now he was inside her head, so was she really feeling these things, or was it just because he wanted her to? Or did he even want her? Was she attractive to him, or did he only like lizard-girls? Her mind reeled, and finally she just put her head between her knees and started to cry.

"What is wrong? Why are you sad?" He sat beside her and put an arm around her shoulders, pulling her face into his chest. Rachel tried to explain what she was feeling, what was going on in her head, but all that came out was broken pieces of words and sentences.

"Billy…Scott…dragon…Dad…helmet…headache…shit…all   so confusing." She cried even harder, then abruptly shoved him away.

Auros stood, looking down at the girl, who sat wiping her eyes with the back of her hand. She looked up at him, her face red and blotchy. "I don't suppose you have a hanky in those swim trunks, do you?"

"No, but I have this." He waved his hand in the air, and a mono-grammed silk handkerchief appeared. He handed it to her.

"That's handy." She wiped her eyes, blew her nose, and started to hand it back to him. Rachel looked at the damp handkerchief and laughed softly. "I guess you probably don't want it back, huh?"

"No. But neither do you." He waved his hand again, and the hand-kerchief vanished. "Now there will likely be a very confused owner of that handkerchief the next time they see it."

"How did you do that?"

"Magic. A simple translocation spell. I think of something I need, and the magic finds it. When I am finished with it, I ask the magic to return it from whence it came, and it goes."

"Did you just use the word 'whence' in a sentence?"

"Yes. Is it not appropriate?"

"How long were you under that mountain before they blew the top off it the other day?"

"I am unsure. I believe, guessing by the amount of growth in the forests on this continent and the rock formations I have glimpsed, that I slumbered for nearly six millennia."

"You were asleep for six thousand years?"

"By my best estimation, yes."

"And you're still alive? How does that work?"

"I am a dragon. We do not die, although we can be killed." His face went somber at that, as though he were remembering something or someone from before he went into hibernation.

"So why are you awake now? I mean, I guess I know. My dad and his crew kinda blew the top off your mountain, and that had to be a rude awakening. But why were you sleeping under a mountain? Are there other dragons asleep down there? Are there dragons pretending to be people?"

The dragon-boy held up a hand, laughing. "Slow down. I am only capable of answering one question at a time. But now I believe we should wait for your male friends to arrive." He stood and walked away from her, and Rachel missed the warmth of his body pressed into her back.

"My what?" Rachel asked, then her eyes widened as she heard a boat motor nearby. A few minutes later, a breathless Scott crashed into the clearing, carrying a baseball bat and followed closely by Billy, who held a hunting knife. The boys almost collided with each other as they took in the sight of Rachel sitting calmly on the boulder, still in nothing but her bikini, with Auros leaning against a tree ten feet away.

"Rachel! Are you okay?" Scott ran to her side, dropping the bat as he ran. He stood her up off the rock and held her shoulders, turning her this way and that, checking for bruises. Billy stood watching, a strange look on his face. He looked at Rachel like he'd eaten something sour.

She shook Scott's hands off and said, "I'm fine, really."

"Who are you?" Billy asked Auros.

"I am Auros," the boy said. Billy stood there, obviously waiting for him to continue, but the dragon-boy was done talking.

Scott finally finished staring at Rachel and took in the clearing. "Where's the dragon? And who's this guy?"

"He's Auros," Rachel and Billy said together. They looked at each other and broke up laughing, suddenly best friends again, with all of Billy's stupidity of the past week forgotten. Scott looked back and forth between them, then walked over to Auros.

"Maybe you can help me…Auros, was it?" Scott turned on the

same charm he used on the guys at the mine, giving the new boy a big smile. Scott leaned against the trunk of a tree like he didn't have a care in the world. As long as you ignored the fact that he'd picked up the baseball bat again and had it leaning against his leg. "You see, me and Billy were having a little disagreement, then we were rudely interrupted by a dragon. Then that dragon snatched my girlfriend up and flew away with her. We followed in my buddy Aaron's boat, and we watched the dragon land somewhere around here. So then we hauled ass through the woods and found you here. With my girlfriend. And no dragon. So I've gotta wonder, where's the dragon?"

"I am right here," Auros said.

"You're the dragon?" Scott said, laughing.

"Yes."

"And I'm supposed to just believe that?"

"Why would I lie?"

"I have no idea, dude. Why would you kidnap my girlfriend and fly off with her?"

"I was protecting her. She had been injured in your foolish scuffle. That caused me pain. I did not enjoy it. So I removed her from the vicinity of the pain."

"What a load of crap. Who are you, and how did you get here?" Billy elbowed his way past Scott and got right up in front of Auros. "I know you're no friggin' dragon, so quit lying to me." He gave the other boy a slight shove, and Auros stumbled back a couple of steps.

Rachel shook her head as Auros began to glow. Like before, it started as a slight golden shimmer, then quickly grew into a blinding light that had them all covering their eyes and looking away. In a few seconds, the light faded, and when the teens looked back, Auros was gone.

In his place was a golden dragon the size of a barn. Billy stood right in front of the creature, looking up, up, up at its head. The long neck writhed, and the head descended. The mouth opened, and Billy looked at more teeth than he could quickly count. "Now do you believe me?" the dragon asked, raising one eyebrow ridge.

Billy scrambled backward, falling to his butt and skittering on all fours. He turned, regained his footing, and started running for the opposite side of the clearing. Rachel jumped up to intercept him, and he stopped before he ran her over. "I might have been mistaken about your friend the great big damn dragon, Rachel. Let's go!"

"He's fine, Preston. Now chill out," Scott said. Scott leaned against a tree, baseball bat down by his side. *He is the perfect picture of nonchalance,* Rachel thought, except maybe the picture was a little *too* perfect. He was a little too calm, a little too together. She gave him a closer look and saw the white knuckles on the bat, the taut muscles vibrating in his legs that were stretched almost to the snapping point.

"Guys, chill," she said. Rachel walked over to the dragon and held out a hand. Auros dropped his head to the forest floor, and she scratched him behind the ears. "See?" she said. "Harmless. Well, at least he doesn't mean us any harm."

"Tell that to the men he killed at the mine! You knew some of those men, Rachel. Your father was almost one of them!" Scott snapped, and Billy nodded.

"I apologize for that. They startled me with their weapons. I was frightened, and I had been awakened mere moments before from a long slumber," the dragon said.

"Yeah, think about it, guys. You know how pissy you are when you first wake up, Billy. Now multiply that by twenty bazillion, and you'll be close to this. He didn't mean to hurt anybody. He was just…you know, startled. And they did kinda shoot him," Rachel said.

Scott stepped forward, placing himself between Rachel and the dragon. "So…Auros…why are you here?"

"I am here because your people awakened me."

"Yeah, I got that. But are you the only dragon, or are the more of you coming?"

The dragon lowered his head, and once again, the golden glow surrounded him, and seconds later, he had assumed the form of a teenage boy again. "This form is more comfortable for you, I believe. And there is much to explain. Please, sit." He sat cross-legged on the forest floor, and the others followed suit.

The dragon took a deep breath and looked at the teens. "What I am telling you is the greatest secret of dragonkind. We have lived for many, many years. Long before man held dominion over the world, dragons ruled the skies. We served the balance of nature, never taking too much from a region before moving on. We worked with the natural ebb and flow of seasons, with the growing and reaping times. We were not alone; we had partners in our endeavors—the elves."

"Elves?" Rachel breathed. "Like real, honest-to-God pointy-eared elves?"

"Yes, real elves. And their ears to come to a point more than humans, but they are very similar in many respects. The dragons and elves ruled the Earth, and we were benevolent rulers. We did not overburden the resources of any one region, but moved from continent to continent in search of ever-greener forests and pastures to hunt and feed from. But in time, there came a great threat to our dominion—humans."

"Humans?" Scott asked. "How are we a threat to something like you?"

"Dragons do not die, but we are born very rarely. If there is one dragon birth in a century, it is cause for celebration. And two? Well, that is unbridled prosperity. Elves are much the same, incredibly long-lived, but incredibly slow to breed as well. And you humans? Well, to say you put rabbits to shame is only a slight exaggeration. In time, the dragons realized that the human population would soon outstrip that of elves and dragons combined, and the world could not sustain the needs of all three races.

"So we went to sleep. The dragons entered hibernation until such time as humanity had eradicated itself. For we knew long ago that the eventual course of mankind is to burn brightly for a short time, but then to flare out like a candle in a hurricane. And we are patient creatures. When one does not die, one needs not hurry."

"You were just going to wait for us to die and then take over the world again?" Rachel asked.

"Exactly. That was the intent of the Council of Dragons. But as the Great Hibernation was to begin, a small faction of traitorous dragons rebelled, slaying the Council and making plans with several rebellious elven leaders to awaken at the height of mankind, instead of after its fall."

"Why? Wouldn't that cause all the problems you wanted to avoid with lack of resources and stuff?" Scott asked.

"Yes, but it would supply the dragons and elves with one resource in abundance—slaves." The teens looked at each other in shock.

Rachel shivered, despite the warmth of the afternoon. "Is that what you think has happened? That the elves are trying to wake the dragons and enslave all the humans?"

"I believe so. I am a very young dragon, barely five hundred years old when I began to slumber. But my mother sat upon the Council, and she taught me much of the leadership of our people. I watched the elves betray her and the other councilors. I watched the traitors among my own people murder our leaders. My own father..." He shook his head. "That is not a tale for now. It is not important. What is important is that the spells were cast, and the Great Hibernation began. When the dragons went into the earth to await the call from the elves to awaken, I remained apart. I did not burrow as deeply into the mountains as my kin, so that I should be the first to wake. And if the treachery was still upon us, to be the first to fight. And now I am awakened, and from what I can judge, the elves are poised to bring forth the dragons and take hold of your people. If the excavation continues where I was found, the dragons will be freed. And that will not go well for mankind."

Billy opened his mouth to speak, but Scott raised a hand to silence him. "Listen." They fell silent for several seconds until the sound of a helicopter became clear. Under the *whup-whup-whup* of the rotors, outboard motors could be heard clearly.

Scott stood up and stepped back into the tree line. "I think we've got company."

Rachel jumped off the rock she was sitting on when a black bag dropped to the ground just a few feet away. Six black bags landed in the clearing, with ropes trailing from them up to a black helicopter that hovered just above the treetops. Men in black helmets, combat boots, and goggles dropped out of the sky, rappelling to the ground face first, then flipping over to land on their feet with machine guns at the ready. They were clad head-to-toe in black combat gear, and no insignia or flag showed anywhere on their uniforms. One stood over each teen, while two trained their weapons on Auros, who sat calmly throughout their entrance.

When the men had secured the teens, another man descended a rope into the clearing. He wore the same combat uniform as the others, but without the helmet, goggles, and face mask. He carried no gun and wore a black cap backward on his head. He was tall, taller than all the other men, but thin, with sharp features and long blond hair swept back into a ponytail. Rachel recognized him instantly—Ted Bentley, the man who had come to her house the day before looking for Auros. *Looks like he's given up pretending to be Mr. Nice Government Guy.* Bentley looked around the clearing and then gestured at the men. They shouldered their weapons, but Rachel noticed none of them took their eyes off their assigned target, nor did they take their fingers away from the triggers.

"Rachel, so good to see you again," the man who introduced himself as Ted Bentley said, in the most obvious lie ever. "Don't worry, children. I'm from the government, and I'm here to help."

CHAPTER 14

Rachel managed not to laugh, which she thought was a good thing since the man did have half a dozen soldiers backing him up. "Great to see you again, Mr. Bentley." *Two can play this whole "kill them with kindness" game.*

Bentley shook her hand and smiled. "I'm sure. Please excuse our entrance. We heard a rumor of a wild animal attack near here and came out to investigate." Rachel figured it was more likely somebody uploaded a video or picture of Auros in dragon form to social media and they traced it back here, but she didn't see any point in saying as much.

"Nope, no wild animals. Unless you count Billy." She smiled and pointed at Billy, who crouched down and did his best monkey impression, which was better than he liked to admit.

"Except for your scaly friend here." Bentley pointed at Auros.

Rachel put on her best innocent face. "I don't know what you mean. 'Eric' there has a little issue with psoriasis, but it's nothing worth calling names over."

"Take them to the boat, and follow them back to the Sandbar. Once they're back with the rest of the kids, initiate the data wipe,"

Bentley said to one of the men with guns. He didn't even acknowledge Rachel's attempt at humor.

"I don't think we're going anywhere until we get some answers, pal." Scott stepped forward, only to find a pair of nasty-looking machine guns pointed at him. There wasn't a whole lot of room for weapons or body armor in his swim trunks, so he put up his hands and backed down. "Fine, whatever. You win."

"You will not speak of this incident again. You will not write anything on your Facebook pages, Twitter, SnapChat, email, or any other type of social media. We will be monitoring these things. This is a matter of national security and will be treated as such. Any disobedience will be met with criminal prosecution. Now you will be returned to the Sandbar safely. Enjoy the rest of your weekend." He turned away from the teens and held out a pair of handcuffs to Auros. "Put these on."

Auros caught Rachel's eye and very deliberately swept his loose blond hair back behind his ears, revealing the pointed tips. She didn't understand what he meant for a minute until she caught sight of Bentley's ears. They had the same points, much sharper and more upswept than normal human ears, and they were completely without earlobes. Bentley was an elf! Rachel's heart raced, but she just nodded to Auros and tried to come up with a plan to free him.

The dragon-boy looked at Bentley and the handcuffs with disdain. "You don't really believe these pitiful bracelets can contain me, do you?"

"Of course they can. Those are cold iron shackles. It is impossible for even you to use magic while wearing them. And you will wear them. Or I will kill you where you stand, and then I will kill every witness here, including the girl. Now put on the shackles." Auros did as he was told.

Bentley nodded to the soldiers, and a pair of them motioned for Rachel and the boys to head into the woods. They did as instructed and walked back through the woods to where Billy and Scott had parked the boat. It felt to Rachel like days had passed since she was quietly fishing with Scott, instead of just a few hours. They got in the boat and headed back to the Sandbar with a pair of black boats as an escort. Each boat held three armed men, and there were two other boats pulled up to the shore. Somehow this Mr. Bentley had mobilized a couple dozen heavily-equipped soldiers or mercenaries in a matter of minutes. Unless they had already been following her. Rachel shivered again at the money and power this man—*no, not man—elf* possessed.

The Sandbar was almost deserted when they returned, the dragon and the soldiers having dampened everyone's mood and sent them all home early. J.C. was there, and Aaron, and a couple of underclassmen sitting around getting tanked on abandoned beer. Aaron hopped in his boat the second they landed and sped off toward home, and Billy got into J.C.'s boat wordlessly and rode off without looking back at Rachel and Scott. The soldiers didn't even beach their boats, just watched the teens land and then turned around to head back to wherever they came from. Rachel wandered around for a few minutes collecting her stuff and putting it onto Scott's boat; then she sat down next to the underclassmen and reached into the cooler for a beer.

"Hey, that's ours!" one freshman boy protested.

Scott walked up behind him, smacked him on the back of the head, and sat down beside Rachel. "Shut up, kid. A lady comes up and wants a beer, you give the lady a beer. Same goes for upperclassmen. Now gimme a beer." The kid complied, then got to his feet and walked over to a little jon boat. He motioned for his buddy to follow, and they were soon rowing off toward home, if not completely steadily.

"Well, I gotta say, as first dates go, this one was certainly exciting," Scott said after a long pull on his beer.

"I'll give you that, Morrison. I've never had a first date quite like this one." She leaned back against his chest and snuggled her head in under his jaw. Scott wriggled around until his back was to one of the more permanent logs half-buried in the sand and put one arm around her.

"So now what?" he asked.

"Now what, what?"

"I know you're not just going to let it go, so you might as well tell me what you've got going on in that adorable little head of yours."

"I don't know, but I know I don't trust that government dude."

"Did he actually ever say he was from the government?" Scott asked.

Rachel thought for a second, took a sip of her beer, and made a face. "How do you drink this stuff? It tastes like crap. And no, I guess he never said he was from the government, except for his lame idea of a joke when he landed, but he certainly implied it."

"Yeah, I know. That's what makes me think he wasn't from the government at all. I've seen my dad deal with those guys at the mine, and they're always waving badges around and telling you exactly what branch they're from and how important they are. This dude didn't do any of that. He just ran us off and took your lizard boyfriend into custody."

"Hey! He's not my boyfriend. He's not a lizard, either. I've got a boyfriend, and he's not the least bit scaly." She wrapped her arms around his arm where it crossed her chest and pulled it close to her. She leaned her head back, and he bent down to press his lips to hers. The kiss started off soft, but deepened quickly. She reached behind him, pulling him close, turning in his grasp until she was sitting in his lap kissing him. His fingers traced fire along her spine, and where his fingers had been, ghost trails of heat remained. It felt like they were glowing in contrast with her cooling skin. His hand curved along her side, reached around, leaving a trail of goosebumps that went straight to her nipple, sending warmth coursing all through Rachel's body. His hand neared her breast, brushing the underside where it played peek-aboo with her bikini top, and she grabbed his wrist.

"Not yet," she said, smiling down at him. Scott groaned in frustration, and she kissed him on the tip of his nose. Rachel hopped off his lap and twirled away from him, grinning as she looked down at the obvious effect she had on him. "I'm not that easy, mister. This is just our first date as boyfriend and girlfriend after all. I can't have you thinking I'm some kind of slut."

"You're a terrible human being, you know that?" Scott got to his knees and adjusted himself in his shorts. Rachel had her bag and was already almost to the boat, so he picked up his t-shirt and his beer and followed her. He had almost reached the girl when she cried out sharply and fell to the sand, both hands clutching her head.

"Rachel!" Scott yelled, crossing the last few feet in one long bound. "What's wrong?" She was lying on the ground, writhing in pain. Her fists beat against the sand and her feet kicked at nothing. Her eyes were squeezed shut, and her mouth opened in soundless screams. Scott wrapped his arms around her, holding her until the fit ended. She shook and convulsed for almost a full minute before her eyes fluttered open.

"S-Scott?"

"I'm here, baby. Are you okay?"

"I think so. Can you get me some water?"

He looked around at the discarded Styrofoam coolers and bags that kids had left when the soldiers landed, finding a fresh bottle of water in one. He held her head as she drank, not trusting her to sit up yet. She gulped the water down like she hadn't had a drink in days, panting when the bottle was finished. Scott lay her on the sand, grabbed another bottle from a different cooler, and settled in next to her.

"Here you go." He handed her the second bottle, and she sucked half of it down greedily. After a few minutes, she seemed to be back to herself, so Scott helped her sit up.

"What happened?" he asked. "If you're epileptic, that's a heck of a way to let a guy know." He laughed as he said it, but it was a hollow laugh, devoid of any humor.

"I'm not. I don't know what that was, it's just all of a sudden there was this incredible pain in my head. Oh my God, it was Auros. It's that psychic link he was talking about." She closed her eyes against the sun and the ache in her temples, and Scott held her close as her shaking subsided.

That was awful, Rachel thought. *I could feel what they were doing to him.* Behind her closed eyes, she relived the images that had just flared across her mind. She saw images of Auros being shackled, bound with those magic-dampening iron handcuffs and thrown into the floor of a helicopter. The man who called himself Bentley grinned down at the dragon-boy and kicked him solidly in the head. That pain was transmitted to Rachel through the healing bond she shared with the dragon, the same way he knew when Billy knocked her down earlier. Rachel didn't know who Ted Bentley really was, but she knew one thing for sure—Auros was in trouble, big trouble, and she was the only one who could help.

"Scott?" Rachel asked.

"Yeah, babe?"

"I think I need your help."

"Anything."

"You might want to hear what it is before you say that." She smiled at him. "What if I asked you to help me rob a bank?"

"I'd say your ski mask or mine?" He smiled down at her.

"Good. Because I think you're right—those guys weren't from the government. I think that Bentley guy was an elf. And I think he's going to hurt Auros unless we rescue him."

"Yeah, I know."

Rachel sat up, shaking her head against the rush of dizziness that threatened to overwhelm her. "What do you mean, you know?"

"I mean I saw the dude's ears. And I told you he wasn't any government goober that I'd ever seen, so it made sense that he was an elf. If anything the dragon told us is true, that is." He finished off his beer in one long swallow and stood up, holding a hand down to her. "Ready to go?"

"Go where?" Rachel took his hand and stood, completely baffled. Scott was pretty unflappable, but this was just plain crazy.

"We're meeting Billy at the high school an hour after dark. We figure if the dragon could track you like a GPS earlier, we can use you the same way to find him."

"When did you even talk to Billy? And when did you two stop hating each other's guts?"

"We whispered a little while you were trying to bluff 'Mr. Bentley' into leaving us alone. We're guys. We can communicate with a couple of grunts and farts."

"But you can't ever ask for directions." Rachel grinned at him and got into the boat. "Well, what are we waiting for? Don't we have a dragon to rescue?"

Scott got into the boat and cranked the engine. He pulled his shirt on and grabbed a baseball cap from under his chair to keep his wild brown curls out of his face while he drove. He pointed the boat back toward the landing and pushed the throttle.

CHAPTER 15

An hour later, they had loaded the boat onto Scott's trailer, deposited the fish into a cooler at his house for cleaning later, and dropped the trailer off in Scott's yard. Rachel had brought a change of clothes, not knowing what the day held, and was glad for the shorts and t-shirt. Her sneakers weren't the best shoes for rescue operations, but it wasn't like she owned a lot of military garb. She made a quick call to her dad when they stopped at Scott's, telling him that they would be pushing curfew a little.

"No, dad, I'm not spending all day and night alone with Scott," she protested. *Not that I'd mind.* "We're meeting Billy and some other folks for pizza in like half an hour. Then we're probably going to hang out in the parking lot over at the high school, or maybe cruise around a little. We won't be on the water, I promise." She knew she wasn't lying. She could sense Auros, and he was nowhere near the lake.

"Fine, but you be careful around that Morrison boy. There were some government men around here today, and they were asking questions about him," her dad said. Rachel's blood ran cold.

"Government men?" she asked. Scott whirled to face her, his mouth open. "What were they asking about Scott for?"

"I have no idea, sweetheart, but they were looking for you, and when I told them you weren't here, they asked if you were with Scott Morrison. They didn't tell me what they wanted, just to have you call them when you got in."

"What branch of government did they say they were with?" Rachel asked.

"You know, that's kind of odd. They didn't say. I have the guy's card here. That's right—Agent Theodore Bentley with the Federal Bureau of Interspecies Relations. Can't say that I've heard of that one, have you? Wonder what the Morrison boy has done…"

"He probably hasn't done anything, Dad. He told me in class yesterday that he was interested in biology, and that sounds like some kind of biology thing—interspecies relationships. Doesn't it?" Her lie sounded feeble even to herself, but somehow her dad bought it.

"Yeah, maybe you're right. Well, I guess it's okay if you're a little late, as long as Billy's with you. Just be home by midnight, and don't go out toilet papering houses or anything like that!" He chuckled.

"Dad! I haven't TP'd a house since eighth grade. It's all Jell-O wrestling from now on!" she teased as she hung up the phone.

"Note to self: stop by grocery store for Jell-O," Scott said with a grin. "Seriously, though. What was that about government guys?"

"Apparently they stopped by my house, asking about you. They claimed to be from the Department of Interspecies Relations."

"Yeah, right. Like human, elf, and dragon relations. I wonder if they came here." He turned to look at his door, and Rachel grabbed his arm.

"If they did, I don't want to think what they told your mother about me. I'm sure she hates me already. I don't need any help from an elf with a fake badge."

"Why would my mother hate you?"

"Because you're her son, and women always hate the girls who date their sons. It's a law. Now can we get the hell out of here before somebody comes out of your house with a bunch of questions we don't want to answer?" She climbed into the truck and looked back at him expectantly.

Scott got in and put the truck in gear, waving at his mother in the kitchen window as he drove past. Rachel's mind raced a million miles an hour as they drove to the school. Where was Auros? Was this Bentley guy really an evil elf? Was Scott going to take her to prom? Would there even be a prom if they couldn't save the dragon?

She flipped on the radio and rolled the window down, letting the cool air run through her hair and the smell of late honeysuckles relax her. She looked over at Scott, driving left-handed and flipping channels on the radio with his right, and thought about how it was an almost perfect day. Well, if you don't count the fight at the Sandbar. And the dragon. And the elves kidnapping the dragon. And having to play commando and rescue the dragon. She smiled, and Scott caught her with a silly grin on her face.

"What's so funny?" he asked, suddenly self-conscious in that adorable way teenage boys have when they think somebody's laughing at them.

"Nothing. I was just thinking, that's all."

"Thinking about what?"

"Thinking how even with all the crazy that today had, and still has, it was a pretty awesome day." She saw him smile, and that honest smile made her flush all the way down to her toes.

"It was pretty cool. You should have seen the way everybody at the 'Bar looked at you." He grinned.

"What? Why were they looking at me? Did my boob fall out and you not tell me? What happened?" Her heart beat faster, and she felt a bead of sweat pop out on her brow as she sat there, thinking this was why she never went out, there were too many people just waiting to pounce on you for the littlest thing, then she saw Scott chuckling at her.

"You really don't know, do you?"

"Know what? What was wrong with me?"

"Nothing. You were the prettiest girl there, and every girl hated you a little bit for it. And every guy hated me. Not as much as Billy Preston, but a little."

"You're full of crap. Jessica Baker is so much prettier than me. And she's got better boobs."

"They're the best boobs money can buy, but she can't hold a candle to you. And she knows it. That's why she doesn't like you. Even under the baggy t-shirts and bike gear you wear, she knows who the competition is."

Rachel opened her mouth to protest, then closed it again with a little smile. If he thought she was awesome, who was she to shatter his illusions? And besides, they were pulling into the school parking lot, and there was Billy. It was time to play ninja and rescue a dragon. Rachel got out of the truck, still a little giggly from the ride, but the smile died on her lips when she saw Billy.

He was dressed like an 80s action-movie star with camouflage pants, black t-shirt, and combat boots. But what worried her more was the pistol on his hip and the shotgun in his hands. Both looked real, and she knew Billy had a short fuse.

"Hey, Billy. What's with the arsenal?" she said, trying to make light of the situation.

"Did you see the guns those guys were packing? Those were MP-5 submachine guns. Serious firepower. If we want to rescue your scaly boyfriend, we're going to need every piece of hardware we can get."

"Okay, one, he's not my boyfriend. Two, we're not going there to kill people, Billy. That's crazy."

"Rachel, it's crazy thinking we can bust into whatever kind of super-prison they've got that dragon buried in, much less get back out again. But if I'm going to do crazy, I'm going to go all the way."

"He's right, Rachel." Scott stepped forward before they moved into the yelling part of the program. "What are you loaded with?" He nodded toward the shotgun.

"Bean bag rounds. This is the gun Mom keeps by the bed for home defense. It most likely won't kill anybody, but it'll put a grown man on his ass for a while. You packing?" He looked past Scott to the truck. Unlike many in their high school parking lot, Scott's pickup had no gun rack in the back window.

"Just this." Scott reached behind the seat and pulled out an aluminum baseball bat. "I don't own a gun."

"And you call yourself a West Virginian." Billy turned back to Rachel. "You said you could find the lizard?" he asked.

"He has a name. He is not a lizard. And yes, I can find him." Rachel was getting tired of Billy's attitude, but she knew they needed him if they were going to get Auros back safely.

"Then let's roll. You get shotgun, and I'll be in the back with the real shotgun." Billy climbed into the back seat of Scott's truck, and they pulled out of the parking lot. Rachel closed her eyes and tried to focus on the dragon.

"Where is he?" Scott asked.

"Hang on. It's not like a GPS. If I concentrate, I can see what he's seeing." She closed her eyes again and felt the link between them strengthen. He opened his eyes, and Rachel looked around at the dragon's surroundings. The feeling was strange, like she was wearing a pair of glasses with the prescription just a little too strong, but she adjusted quickly.

"He's in a motel. I can see the crappy bedspreads, the little round table by the window, the bathroom off to one side. He's gotta be at the Mountainview."

"Is there anybody in the room with him?" Billy asked.

"One guard. He thinks there's another outside by the door, but that's all he knows. Bentley is nowhere around."

"You can read his mind, too?" Scott asked.

"It's not like mind-reading, I don't think. It's more like a walkie-talkie. I can talk to him a little, and he can talk to me a little, but it's not like I can tell what he's thinking. He can just send me messages and stuff."

"How did this happen?" Scott put the truck into gear and pulled out of his parking space.

"When I got knocked silly at the Sandbar, he healed me. When he did, our essences mingled somehow, and now our minds are linked."

"I'm not going to comment on you mingling essences with another guy," Scott said, the corner of his mouth twitching up. Billy snorted behind her, burying his laughter in his hand.

Rachel punched him in the shoulder. "Shut up. It's bad enough I have a dragon in my head, I don't need a bunch of crap about it from you two clowns."

"Freaky," Billy said from the back seat. Scott turned left out of the school parking lot and headed out of town.

The Mountainview Inn was the lone motel in town, and all the kids at school knew where it was. A long single-story structure with rooms that opened out onto the parking lot, The View, as it was often called, had been the site of many after-prom parties and many high school boys' conquests over the years. Old Mrs. Gromwell, the live-in daytime manager, had a strict policy of no one under eighteen renting rooms. Lucky for the local teens that Willie Bransome, the night manager, had no such policy and would rent a room to as many Mr. & Mrs. Smiths as wanted to pay cash for a room. It also helped that Mrs. Gromwell was almost completely deaf and blind and never came out of her room once the sun went down.

Scott pulled off the road a quarter-mile from the hotel and opened his door. He got out, and the other teens followed suit. "Why are we stopping here?" Rachel asked.

"The parking lot is gravel and noisy as hell. I'm not worried about Old Lady Germwell, but if there is a guard outside, I don't want him to see or hear us pull up. We'll walk from here and take the front. Billy will go around by the creek and come in off the balcony. Since he's dressed like Rambo, I figured we'd let him play Rambo."

"Works for me. Rachel, does Scaly-boy know if there's anybody else in the motel, or is he in the only occupied room? Otherwise, I won't know which balcony to storm."

"He doesn't know if there's anybody else in the motel, but he says the sliding door out onto the balcony is open, and his guard keeps going outside to smoke. That should help, right?"

"That's all I need. Synchronize watches?" Billy asked.

"Nah, just come over the rail when you hear the racket," Scott said.

"Deal." The boys fist-bumped, and Billy headed off into the woods.

"We'll give him a couple minutes' head start and then make our move."

"And what is our move, exactly?" Rachel asked.

"Do you still have on your bikini bottoms?" Scott asked with a grin.

CHAPTER 16

Ten minutes later Rachel was walking along the sidewalk in front of the motel with her t-shirt pulled down as far as is it would go over her ass and a vapid smile on her face. She walked slowly up to the guard standing outside Room 9 and leaned into him. "Hey there," she said with a lazy smile.

He looked up and down the sidewalk as if he wasn't sure she was talking to him, then took a long look at the half-naked teenager standing before him. He smiled back at her, giving her bare legs the once-over, then the twice-over. "Hey, yourself," he replied.

"Do you know where the ice machine is?" Rachel purred, then stretched languorously, her arms high above her head.

"Yeah, it's a couple doors down." The guard pointed toward the office. Rachel could see light spilling out of an open doorway.

"Thanks. My boyfriend and I rented a room for the weekend. The sound of the stream behind the rooms sounds so romantic. But now we're out of ice, and I want to play some more." She turned away, then froze. She turned back to the guard, eyes wide.

"I forgot my ice bucket. Can I borrow yours?" She strutted back to where he stood, looking confused.

"I'm sorry, miss. I can't open the door for anyone but my boss."

"Oh well, I guess I'll just have to carry ice in my shirt, then." She gave him another sly grin and reached for the hem of her t-shirt. The guard's eyes went wide, then turned glassy as Scott clubbed him behind the ear with the baseball bat.

"I was wondering how naked you were going to make me get," Rachel said, grabbing her shorts from Scott.

"Sorry, got distracted. And we can talk about getting you naked later. When there aren't as many guns around." He grinned at her and rolled the guard over. "Help me check this guy's pockets. There should be a key card here somewhere." They checked all his pockets, but came up empty.

"Nothing," Rachel whispered.

"They probably use a passphrase on the door," Scott said.

"Just bang on the door and say you've gotta pee."

Scott nodded at her and pounded on the door. "Lemme in," he said, pitching his voice lower and gruffer.

"What's the password?" came the answer from within.

"Come on man, I gotta use the bathroom!"

"That ain't the password." The voice on the other side of the door was sing-song, like a guy teasing his buddy. "Just pee in the parking lot. It ain't like there's anybody around to see ya."

"I ain't gotta pee, man. It's the other!"

"What?" came the voice on the other side of the door.

"I gotta drop some kids off at the pool, now open the damn door!"

"Oh. Why didn't you say you had to crap?" The door opened a crack, and Scott threw it the rest of the way open, catching the guard in the face. Scott bulled his way into the room and looked across the small hotel room. Billy was climbing over the balcony rail outside, and Auros was handcuffed on the double bed farthest from the door. The guard was recovering quickly, and Scott jammed the baseball bat into his stomach. His body armor protected him from the worst of the blow, and he scrambled to bring his gun up.

A thunderous boom shook the entire room, and the guard flew forward, crashing into Scott as he dropped, face-first onto the carpet. Rachel froze in the doorway and stared at Billy, standing in the sliding doorway with a smoking shotgun. "Holy crap, Billy! Did you kill him?"

"Nah. Like I said, bean bag rounds. Might have cracked a rib or two, but that's it. Let's see if he's got the keys to the cuffs." Billy carefully leaned the shotgun against a wall and started to search the groaning guard. He quickly disarmed the man and bound his hands and feet with plastic zip-ties that were hanging from his belt. Scott dragged the other guard into the room and shut the door, then dumped the unconscious man on the empty bed. He took all his weapons away, then trussed him up like Billy had done with his prisoner. Scott searched both guards and took the batteries out of their radios and cell phones, then dropped all the devices in the back tank of the motel toilet.

He came back into the room, wiping his hands on his jeans. "I don't even want to think about the last time that thing was cleaned."

"No keys," Billy reported. Rachel just grinned at the boys and reached into the pocket of her shorts, which she had put back on after taking out the guard. She pulled out a bobby pin and sat on the edge of the bed next to Auros. He was still dressed only in yellow swim trunks, and the feeling of that much skin pressed up against her stirred some uncomfortable feelings in Rachel. *You're Scott's girl now. Don't even think about it. But he's soooo pretty.* She shook her head and focused on the matter at hand. In a few seconds, she had the cuffs off and Auros was standing.

"How did you learn that little trick?" Scott asked.

"I had a magic kit in Arizona. There weren't many kids for me to play with, so I practiced escape tricks. You get yourself locked in the handcuffs often enough, you learn how to get out of them." Her faced turned beet-red as she thought about what she'd just said. "Never mind."

"Thank you. All of you. I did not dare hope that you would come for me," Auros said. He shimmered for a second, then a set of dark clothes appeared around him.

"No man left behind, brother." Billy clapped him on the shoulder and gave him a shove toward the door. "Now let's get out of here before your pointy-eared friend gets back."

"He is not my friend. I do not like him at all." Auros followed Billy out the door, looking a little confused. "Why would you call him my friend?"

"Rachel, you get to sit in the back with the lizard and teach him about sarcasm," Billy said. Scott laughed, and they ran out of the hotel and back to the truck.

Forty-five minutes later, they were bouncing along an unmarked, unpaved road as Scott navigated apparently by feel. Rachel had no idea how he could see anything in the pitch blackness that crowded around the truck. Tree branches scraped across the roof of the truck and flapped into the open windows, sending Rachel diving onto Auros' lap to keep from getting smacked in the face.

"Sorry," she said, her hand pressed against the dragon-boy's muscular chest.

"I do not mind. I would hate for you to be injured because of me." He smiled at her, and Rachel felt a warmth burning in her chest. She turned away, rolling the window up and hiding her face. Not for the first time she cursed her pale complexion and the way she blushed at *everything*. She could never hide her feelings from anyone, not even when she didn't understand them, like now. She was Scott's girl, so why was she getting all worked up just riding close to the good-looking blond boy? Was it because she knew he was really a dragon and could kill them all with a blast of fire? Or was it because he had abs for days and eyes you could just fall into and lose yourself and not even care?

Rachel shook herself, then leaned forward between the two front seats. "Scotty, baby. I hate to be a pest, but...where the hell are we going? We must be halfway to Ohio by now."

"You'll see." He smiled at her in the rearview mirror. "Now you might want to put your seatbelt on. I think it's going to get bumpy ahead."

Rachel leaned back and pulled on her seatbelt. If Scott didn't think it was bumpy *now,* she was definitely going to need the restraint. Besides, it gave her something to do instead of smacking Scott on the back of the head or ogling the dragon in the seat next to her.

Scott navigated the bumpy road, if you could call it that, for another fifteen minutes before they came to a small turnout. A clear space about thirty feet around had been carved out of the wilderness, smoothed over somewhat with gravel, but the road dead-ended here. Scott pulled the truck off to one side of the clearing and shut it off.

"Okay, we're here. There might be swimming involved," Scott said, getting out of the truck.

"Swimming?" Rachel asked. "Scott, what are you talking about?" She opened the back door and slid to the gravel.

"Come with me, I'll show you. But everybody watch your step." He grabbed a flashlight from a pocket in the door of his pickup and led her out of the clearing. The ground swiftly turned into an embankment, and Rachel grabbed Scott's arm to keep her balance. They walked a few feet, then came out on the shore of the lake. Scott played his flashlight out across the water, and Rachel recognized the raft where they had spent part of the afternoon.

"Oh, Scott, this is brilliant! Nobody will think to look for him here because—"

"Because nobody else knows about this spot," he finished. "Did I do good? Do I get a prize?" He put his arms around her, and Rachel looked up into his eyes. For a moment, there was no one else around. No Billy, no Auros, no government elf-ninjas coming after them, nothing. Just Scott's two arms around her and his lips pressing into hers. The soft sound of the water lapping against the shore blended with a symphony of crickets and frogs as Rachel lost herself in his kiss. She pulled him closer to her, and he put a hand on her shoulder, pushing her back gently.

Scott looked down into her eyes, smiling at the little pout she put on. "Later, I promise. Right now, I've got to get this dragon hidden on the raft and get you home before your dad sends a posse after me. It's almost eleven, and he wants you home by midnight."

Reality came crashing down around Rachel, and she tried to hide her disappointment. "Okay, but you better plan on one hell of a good-night kiss."

Scott grinned down at her. "I've been planning on that since I picked you up this morning."

"Hey!" Billy's voice floated down to them from the clearing. "You two gonna come up for air? We kinda need to get this lizard secured before sunrise!"

Scott and Rachel walked back up to the clearing, where Auros and Billy waited. "Here's the plan," Scott said to Auros. "There's raft in this cove down there that you can hide on until we get clear of Bentley. I'll talk to my dad tomorrow about not starting up the mine again for a few days, out of respect for the families of the deceased, but that's not going to buy us much time. The mine will be up and operational again by Wednesday, I'm sure of it."

"We cannot allow that to happen," Auros said. "The other dragons slumber barely a hundred feet below where I took my rest. If they are awakened, dark days for all men will be upon us."

"Well, we've got a couple of days, then I'd be surprised if they weren't drilling hundreds of feet down to see how much more mountain has to be removed to get to the coal," Scott said.

"So we have to convince your dad to stop digging for coal in two days?" Billy asked.

"Yeah, in one of the richest coal seams to be found in West Virginia in a hundred years. You can guess how that's gonna go over."

"Probably better than getting any more of his people killed by a pissed-off dragon!" Rachel said. "Now get Auros hidden, and we can deal with the other stuff in the morning. Because if I don't get home by midnight, there might as well not *be* a tomorrow."

Scott motioned for Auros to follow him, and the dragon started toward the water. He stopped in front of Rachel. "Thank you for coming to my aid. It reminds me of the bond we once shared with the elves, the friendship my people held with that species before they grew power-hungry and corrupt. I will not forget your kindness."

Rachel hugged the dragon-boy, taking a moment to feel his hard muscles beneath her. She pulled back and said, "You're welcome. Now go with Scott, and we'll come by tomorrow and make a plan. Okay?"

"Okay. I will see you on the morrow." He followed Scott into the woods, and a few minutes later, Rachel heard a splash.

"On the morrow," Billy mocked, pitching his voice higher than normal. "What a fairy."

"No, dumbass, he's a dragon. I'm pretty sure fairies are smaller," Rachel said. She got in the passenger seat of the truck and stared out at the darkness waiting for Scott to come back. A minute or two later, she saw the beam of his flashlight come bobbing up the trail. Scott reached the truck at a jog and hopped behind the wheel.

"Let's roll, Preston! Rachel's got a curfew she never told me about!" Scott said to Billy, still standing outside the truck leaning on Rachel's open window.

"I didn't think I'd need to when you picked me up *at ten this morning*," the girl replied.

"Fair enough. But let's get you home before your dad has a legitimate reason to hate me."

"I can give him a list if you'd like, Morrison," Billy said, pulling the back door closed. Scott turned the truck around and headed out, moving faster this time. Rachel fastened her seatbelt with fumbling fingers, trying to jam the buckle closed as she bounced around the cab. They were back to the main road in five minutes, and Scott floored it to the high school, where he dropped Billy off at his truck.

"Meet you tomorrow to talk about the lizard?" he asked Rachel.

"Yeah. Call my cell and we'll figure out where to meet. Thanks for your help tonight."

"Anything for you, Rache. Except if it involves helping your dingleberry boyfriend." He gave Scott the finger and got into his truck.

Scott returned the gesture and put his truck in drive, heading for Rachel's house as fast as he could safely drive. "I really got a lotta love for that guy, you know."

"He's not that bad."

"No, he's not that bad, just hates my guts and wants to watch me die in a fiery car crash."

"Don't forget he's had a crush on your girlfriend since the day she moved here." Rachel smiled.

"Wow, aren't we modest?"

"Trust me, it's nothing to brag about. I like Billy, he's been there for me a lot of times when nobody at school would even give me the time of day. But..." She trailed off, looking out the window at her reflection.

"But he's just not what you're looking for?" Scott prompted.

"Yeah. Something like that. I don't know. He's just not what I want in a boyfriend."

"Glad to hear it." Scott grinned at her. Rachel gave him a smile, and they drove the rest of the way to her house in an easy silence.

They pulled up in front of her house, and Rachel looked at her watch. "11:57. Not bad. And I don't think you broke any world records getting me home."

"Then I'll try harder next time." Scott opened his door and walked around to open the passenger door for Rachel. He stood there for a moment, not quite letting her out of the truck, then leaned in and kissed her. Unlike their earlier kisses, this one had an urgency behind it that made Rachel tingle all the way down to her toes. She wrapped her arms around his neck and kissed him back, trying to convey everything the day had been in just a brief moment of contact.

Scott broke the kiss and pulled back, looking deep into her eyes. Rachel looked up at him, nodded, and slid out of the truck. "Thanks. For everything. It was an awesome first date." Then she gave him a grin and ran up the steps to the porch. "Pick me up at ten tomorrow? I think there might still be a fish in that lake."

"You've got a deal. And maybe this time no swat-ninjas on the Sandbar."

"Sorry to be the deal-breaker, young lady, but you've got church in the morning. And homework. And I need your help around the house tomorrow afternoon. So tell the nice boy you'll see him at school

Monday and then head on inside." Rachel whirled around to see her father sitting quietly in the rocker on the porch. She looked back at Scott, gave him a "what can you do?" shrug, and ran inside. She ran up the stairs to her room, then tiptoed back down to the living room and hid on the sofa so she could eavesdrop.

"Come here, son. Have a seat," her dad's voice said. He sounded remarkably calm, so maybe he wasn't going to murder anyone. Rachel heard a creak as Scott sat on the porch swing. She heard the steady *crick-creeeeak* of the chain as Scott began to slowly rock back and forth.

"Good evening, Mr. Hampton. How are you?"

"I'm fine, Scott. But more importantly, how's Rachel's flossing?" Rachel blushed. She could almost hear the sly grin on her dad's face. Scott was not ready for that level of verbal sparring. This was not going to go well for Team Boyfriend.

"Huh? I mean, um…huh?"

"Well, since she had her tonsils out when she was eight, I figured you were doing some kind of advanced dental exam there in the truck. So how are her teeth?"

"Oh. Oh! They're…nice, very nice, sir. Look, I'm sorry we cut it a little close with the curfew thing, but really, we didn't do anything bad, or wrong, or anything." *Unless you count rescuing a mythical creature from soldiers working under the orders of another mythical creature, but we did that to save the world from enslavement to elves, so it's okay,* Rachel thought. Then she thought that maybe Scott's terror of her father might freeze his vocal chords, and that could be a good thing.

"Well, that's good. I heard there was a little scuffle at the Sandbar today. You and Duke Prescott's boy?"

"Well, yes, sir. Billy and I kinda got into it a little. I think he's upset that Rachel is going out with me instead of him. I'm not going to get into a lot of who started it BS, but we were both kinda stupid, and I'm glad nobody got hurt."

"That's good, son. I don't care who started it, I just don't want Rachel to get hurt in any of that crap. You understand me?"

"Yes, sir. I don't want to see Rachel get hurt in anything."

"Then we're in agreement. And you'll understand that if you hurt my little girl, I'll find the deepest, darkest mine shaft on that mountain to drop your worthless ass down."

"Yes, sir."

"Good, then. Glad we had this talk. Have a nice night." Rachel buried her face in the sofa to keep from screaming or laughing, she wasn't sure which. The idea of her dad actually hurting anyone was ridiculous, but the fact that he'd just *threatened* Scott was infuriating.

She heard Scott's boots clump down the porch steps. Then she heard him get in the truck, crank it up, and leave. Her dad never moved, never twitched. Just sat there watching the truck drive off, then turned his head and spoke to the window. "You can come out now, Rachel."

She got up, walked out the screen door, and sat on the porch swing recently vacated by her boyfriend. "Sometimes you're a real asshole. You know that?"

Her dad smiled at her. "I didn't bring out the shotgun. That should count for something."

"It does. I'm not sure what, but it counts for something. And what was that crap about church? We haven't gone to church since I was nine."

"But your little friend doesn't know that. And I bet you double or nothing on this week's allowance that he'll be front and center at whatever church he doesn't usually go to tomorrow morning looking for you."

Rachel laughed in spite of herself. "That's evil."

"That's parenting. Now, how was your day, dear?"

Rachel thought about the fishing, the swimming, the kissing, the fight, the dragon, the more kissing, the rescue, the more kissing, and tried to decide what to tell her father and how to skip the parts he really shouldn't know about. She drew a breath to answer, and he held up a hand.

"Don't bother. I can see it on your face. You like him, huh?"

Rachel tried to put it into words, and failed. "Yeah."

"I've been waiting years for this day to come, hoping it wouldn't and knowing it would. Just be careful, sweetheart. He does seem like a nice boy. I'd hate to have to throw him down a mineshaft."

Ben Hampton stood up and limped into the house. Rachel sat there for a few more minutes, looking out at the stars and reliving certain moments of the day. Then she stood and went inside with a smile stretching her face tight and went upstairs to dream of pretty boys and even prettier dragons.

CHAPTER 17

"This is not the level of performance I expect from my field operatives." The voice on the phone was calm, too calm.

"I understand, My Lord." The man called Ted Bentley started to kneel by force of habit, then caught himself. *He's not here, idiot. He can't see you.*

"You may kneel, Silvaren. Feel free to supplicate yourself before me as you grovel for my forgiveness."

Bentley/Silvaren knelt on the plush carpet of his office, high above downtown Charleston, and said nothing. Surrounded by expensive leather and dark wood furnishings, the gleaming oak conference table was the centerpiece of the room. In the center of the conference table was a speakerphone with one line lit up. The rest of the office was barely visible in the predawn glow, but the sun was peeking over the mountaintops, and the windowed walls would soon fill the room with light. Light that couldn't touch the black anger filling every corner of Bentley/Silvaren's heart.

His thoughts raced as his master's silence lay heavy across the tele-phone line. *Thousands of years patiently waiting. Centuries of searching for The Hidden Ones. Decades of work in this sickening wasteland of a city and just as I'm about to succeed, I'm thwarted by an upstart dragon and a couple of human whelps? This shall not stand.* "I swear, My Lord, if you but give me one more chance, I will bring the dragon back to the place of Awakening and complete the ritual. These humans cannot stand before our strength and cunning."

"They have…spirit, Silvaren. Spirit and far greater numbers than we. You would do well not to underestimate them. Again."

"I shall not, My Lord. I will approach using the girl-child's father. He is distrustful of the boy, and of the Morrison boy's father—"

"As he should be," the voice on the phone said with a tiny chuckle, the first sound Silvaren had heard all morning that wasn't shot through with anger and disgust.

"I will use that suspicion to gain his trust. The enemy of my enemy is my friend, and all that human claptrap."

"Yes, Silvaren. That should do nicely. What these mortal fools do not understand is that often the enemy of your enemy is just a greater predator. Do not fail me again. I will not be so…understanding." The light on the phone blinked out as the connection was severed from the other end. Silvaren knelt on the carpet for a moment, gathering his thoughts, then with a deep breath, he stood.

Now fully disguised again in the mien of Ted Bentley, Special Agent for the Department of Interspecies Relations, Silvaren walked to his desk and pressed a button on his other phone.

"Yes, Mr. Bentley?" a female voice answered.

"Is this Sheila?" Bentley asked, his tone all honey and good cheer.

"Sherry, Mr. Bentley. Sheila comes on at eight," was the good-natured response.

I should force them to all have the same name. It's so tiresome learning the names these sheep give each other. "Sherry, darling, please have a car sent around. I believe I have to take another trip out to the mine this morning and see what's taking so long on those repairs."

"Will do, Mr. Bentley. Would you like a change of clothes in the car? Wouldn't want to get your suit dirty."

No, you stupid cow, that's why I use magic to keep the filth of your world from touching my person. "Of course, my dear. That's a brilliant idea. Thank you so much!" Bentley closed his eyes as he disconnected the intercom and massaged his temples. *This facade makes me tired. Soon I will no longer have to pretend that these humans are anything more than what they are—cattle to do my bidding or be destroyed. Perhaps I'll feed Sherry? Sheila? Whatever her name is. Perhaps I'll feed her to a dragon and watch the beast devour her.*

His headache gone, Bentley picked up a card from his desk and examined it as he waited for his car to be brought from the garage. "Benjamin Hampton, Head Geologist. And a good morning to you, Mr. Hampton. I'll see you very soon."

CHAPTER 18

The landscape ran like a river, far, far below. The sky was a painted azure canopy dotted with pink, white, and steel-gray clouds. Light reflected off his golden wings, throwing sparkles through the air and dancing along the perfectly toned scales of Azula's thighs and legs as he strove to catch her. Her azure scales bounced yellow sunbeams into blue, dazzling his heart along with his eyes as he gazed upon the perfection that was his love, his heart, his mate.

They flew like that for hours, over hill and stream, over mountain and meadow, over town and desert. Finally, after hundreds of miles, Azula turned in midair, opened her wings to their widest, and beckoned to him. Auros sped into her, sweeping up from below as her change in angle sent her rushing to the ground, and they came together with a crash of scale and light and magic.

Their mating sent them hurtling up where the air was thin, higher than either of them had ever flown before. Then they dove, still joined together by lust and love and hunger, their necks entwined into one long, sinuous neck, their souls touching to form one thought, one sense, one *being*. They splashed deep into the ocean and dove, dove, dove into the depths where their cousins, the sea monsters, frolicked and the only light was the flicker of the fishes until finally the pressure was too great and they shot to the surface, breaking the waves in a froth of seafoam and sweat and love.

Still joined, they flew, blending consciousness, mixing awareness, becoming one in all ways. Their flesh was joined, their minds touched, their souls held each other close. And finally, when their bodies were totally spent from the love they had shared, they landed on an outgrowth of rock far from any dragon, elf, or animal and wound together like one continuous piece of thick blue-and-gold-scaled wire where they slept the sleep of true lovers.

CHAPTER 19

Rachel sat bolt upright in bed, a loud gasp escaping from her lips as she tried to fill her empty lungs. *Holy shit, what was that? That was the hottest sex dream I've ever had, and I don't even think it was mine.* She looked around the room, embarrassed for what she knew intellectually was no good reason, then got up and headed to the bathroom to get a shower and try to wash away the feeling of golden scales rubbing against her tender human flesh.

Later, with her teeth brushed and all thoughts of dragons pushed firmly to the background, Rachel bounded down the stairs to the living room, coming to a sudden halt at the bottom of the stairs as a familiar face smiled up at her. Rachel, clad in her normal Sunday morning apparel of a vintage Rolling Stones concert t-shirt and cut-off jeans, felt suddenly underdressed as Ted Bentley smiled up at her from the foyer by her front door.

"Well, well. Rachel, isn't it? Ted Bentley, FBIR. We met the other day." The elf held out his hand as though he'd never jumped out of a helicopter with a strike team to kidnap a dragon right in front of her.

For her part, Rachel skipped down the last two steps and held out her hand to the elf, just like she'd never helped a dragon escape from government agents and said, "Yes, of course. Good to see you again,

Mr. Bentley. Did you find your anomaly?" She leaned on the banister, smirking a little.

Bentley's smile never touched his eyes. "We did, but someone seems to have made it disappear again. Have you heard anything about that? I know how you kids like to get up to your hijinks." His voice had a false joviality to it, like beating up federal agents was just shenanigans, like TPing someone's house or playing Ding-Dong-Dash on their porch.

"Gee whiz, Mr. Bentley. I don't know anything about disappearing anomalies. But if I hear anything, I'll tell Pop right away, so he can call you," Rachel said in her best *Leave it to Beaver* imitation. She slid past Bentley and headed for the kitchen. "I'm making breakfast, Dad. Omelets for two, or three?" *Please say two, please say two, please say two, please say two.*

"Two, please. I was just leaving. Mr. Hampton, if you think of any place this monster could be hiding, either on mine property or in the surrounding areas, please get in touch with me immediately. As you can see from the photos I shared, this beast is incredibly dangerous." Bentley was back in his "Man in Black" routine, and he slipped on a pair of dark sunglasses to complete the image as he stepped out the front door onto the porch.

"I'll call, Mr. Bentley. Remember, I've seen what that thing can do up close and personal. Those poor men." Her father shook his head as he closed the door behind Bentley. Rachel relaxed a bit as the sound of a Suburban cranking came through the open kitchen window.

"What did he want?" Rachel asked, setting two glasses on the kitchen table and pouring them full of orange juice.

"He needs my help finding his 'anomaly'." Her father came into the kitchen and took two plates out of the cupboard and put them on the table. They moved with the grace that only comes from living with someone else for years, no wasted movement in setting the table, delivering the food from skillet to plate just as the plate hits the table, putting out just the right amount of toast without asking: the little signals the two had developed in the years without Rachel's mother.

"You're not going to help him, are you?" Rachel sat down and tucked into her omelet without looking up at her father.

"Of course I am. That thing is dangerous, no matter what it is. It killed Ed up at the mine, and three federal agents last night when it escaped from captivity. That's enough proof for me—it needs to be destroyed."

"Wait a minute, nobody got killed last—" Rachel cut herself off with a manufactured coughing fit as she realized what she'd almost said. As she got her breathing under control, she was almost overtaken again, this time by a real panic attack. *If those men were alive when we left, then there's just one other person who knew where to find them. Nobody knew they were at the motel except for us and Bentley. He must have* — Rachel cut off her own train of thought and looked up.

"May I be excused? Something isn't agreeing with my stomach." Her father nodded, then looked after her concerned as she bolted past him and threw up noisily in the guest bathroom.

～

"And then he had his own people killed for losing Auros and to make him look like some kind of dangerous beast," Rachel said into her cell phone the next morning as she struggled into her shoes.

Scott's voice came over the line, surprisingly clear given the service and the terrain. Cell phone coverage was spotty in their part of West Virginia, between the mountains and the mineral deposits messing things up.

"We don't know that, Rachel—" Scott started, but Rachel cut him off.

"Wanna bet? I recognized the watch on one guy's wrist. It was the only thing I *could* recognize, Scott! They burned these guys to a crisp just so they could blame it on Auros! And my dad believed them! This is the worst thing in the world." She flopped down on her back on her bed and stared up at the ceiling.

"No, Rache, the worst thing in the world would be if they caught

Auros. At least if what he told us is true." Scott sounded calmer than anyone should under the circumstances, and it just made Rachel angrier.

"What do you mean, *if* what he told us is true? Why would he lie?" *I'm not even sure he* can *lie to me anymore, now that I'm kinda in his head.* That thought brought the feelings from her dream rushing back, and she shook her head as if to banish those images to the background. *Not now, horndog. Deal with your repressed hormones and hot boys after you make sure the dragon is safe.*

"I don't know, Rachel, but why would Mr. Bentley lie? What if he really is from the government? Do you know anybody else with black helicopters?"

"Scott, until yesterday I would have said *nobody* has black helicopters, that they were just stories the 9/11 conspiracy nuts made up. And last week I would have told you that dragons were something out of a storybook, and that elves were just another way for boys to lust after Liv Tyler! But all those things are real, and now this jerkoff has my dad getting ready to go hunt a dragon, and I don't know what to do!" Her voice went high and thready and almost broke, but she managed to pull it together right at the last second.

"I know what you're going to do, young lady." Rachel looked up at the sound of her father's voice. He was standing just inside the bedroom door looking down at her. "You're going to tell Scott good-bye, come out here, and have breakfast with your old man. Then we're going to talk about dragons and black helicopters and elves and what does and does not exist. Then we're going to talk about breaking and entering, and assault, and interfering with a government investigation and how a semester at Guantanamo Bay looks on a college application."

"Shit, Scott. I gotta go. My dad's decided on an interrogation with breakfast. You figure out what to do about this mess, and I'll call you later." Her father grabbed the phone before she could click the "Off" button.

"No, she won't, Scott. She'll see you tomorrow at school. Have a good day at church." He clicked the phone off and walked off.

Rachel washed her face, then her hands, then her face again, then finally decided that she couldn't put it off any longer and went into the kitchen where her father sat at the head of the table. A plate of half-eaten omelet and bacon sat in front of Rachel's chair, and she sat, reaching for the pitcher of orange juice as she did so. Her father just stared at her, the stark white bandages on his hand conspicuous against the flowered tablecloth.

"Well?" he said after watching Rachel eat for several long moments.

"Deep subject, Dad." Rachel grinned at him with the bad pun, but her father's eyes didn't even crinkle. "Okay, I might have met your Mr. Bentley yesterday."

"And...?" It always amazed Rachel how much weight her father could put into one little word. She stared at her bacon, but her father's burned hand lay there, just inside her peripheral vision, almost like it was accusing her.

"And there might have been a guy there..."

"Scott, I assume." Her father's voice was clipped and tight, like when he spoke to her mother on the rare occasions she bothered to make contact.

"Well, yeah, Scott was there, and Billy, and a bunch of kids from school, really..."

"But that's not the boy you mean."

"Well, no. You see, the other day, when I was riding through the woods, I might have accidentally stumbled upon this guy, and his name is Auros, and he's a boy, and he's really pretty, and blond, and built like a brick—"

"Ahem." Her father cleared his throat and Rachel's runaway train of thought screeched to a halt.

"Um, never mind."

"Yes, please, let's never mind that part of it." Her father looked at least twenty percent as uncomfortable as Rachel felt, so she decided to just let that lie and move on.

"Well, turns out that Auros is only a hot boy some of the time, and the rest of the time he's kind of...a dragon. And there might have been a fight at the Sandbar because Billy got jealous of Scott, and Auros might have flown in and made a whole thing out of it, and there might have been men with black helicopters, and one of them might have been your friend Mr. Bentley, and they might have kinda kidnapped Auros."

"So the men from the FBIR came in and captured the anomaly."

"Dragon."

"I am far more comfortable keeping a few minor half-truths in place for right now, young lady."

"So that's kinda what happened yesterday afternoon." Rachel looked anywhere but at her father.

"And what happened last night? Since I seem to recall you being out until the very moment of your curfew."

"Dad! I thought we agreed we had a strict 'don't ask, don't tell' policy about my dating."

"That was when I thought you were keeping it in the species, dear. Now, about last night?"

"Well, the government men might have taken Auros to a hotel, and we might have had something to do with his escape."

"And the burning to death of half a dozen federal agents?" Her father pushed food around on his plate, but didn't take a bite. His eyes never left hers, even when a sausage link escaped the plate and rolled to the floor.

"Not us. Total bullshit. They were fine when we left. A little bruised maybe, but not crispy. That's why I was saying that your pal Bentley is a bad dude. He must have burned up his own men when he found Auros gone to make it look like a dragon attack and cover up his own incompetence."

"You watch too many spy movies. And let's rein in the language a little bit. We are still at the breakfast table."

"Don't be a Puritan."

"Don't talk like a trollop."

"I don't even know what a trollop is."

"I'm sure you can extrapolate from my tone and the disapproving expression. See?" Ben pointed at his knit brow and almost fake scowl.

He relaxed the face, but kept a steady gaze on her. "Really? Black heli-copters, secret rescue operations? How am I supposed to believe all of this, Rachel? You're sixteen, for God's sake. You haven't even lost your virginity; how could you be playing Jason Bourne with a dragon?" Her father paused. "You *haven't* lost your…"

"This is not a conversation we are having over cold omelets, but yes, I am still a virgin. And what exactly are you, the guy who was burned by a dragon a couple of days ago, going to call BS on? The black helicopters? Because I just want to refer back to Exhibit A, the *dragon*." She leaned back in her chair and crossed her arms, affecting what she called Smug Teen Look #3, one of a host of expressions she trotted out whenever she really wanted to get her dad wound up.

He didn't bite. His face held the same serious expression he'd been wearing ever since cutting off her conversation with Scott. "I'm not sure what that thing was, but I know that I don't want you anywhere near it. It killed a good friend of mine and could have killed me. So why don't you forget anything about going out dragon-riding, or whatever you had planned for the day, and concentrate on homework, and yard work, and housework, and any other kind of busy work I can think of to keep you occupied until well past dark. Because for today at least, if not the next ten years, I'm not letting you out of my sight."

Her father was as good as his word. He kept her alternating between cleaning, studying, and doing whatever else he could think of all day and what felt like half the night. By the time he gave her cell phone back and pointed her up the stairs to her room, Rachel could think of nothing but a shower and sleep.

A hot shower relaxed her tired muscles, but sleep wouldn't come. Rachel lay on her bed staring up at the ceiling, her mind whirling. Scott, Auros, Billy, Bentley, the Sandbar, the fight at the motel, the video of the mine—all these things kept spinning through the movie in her mind until finally she drifted off to sleep well after midnight.

CHAPTER 20

"You know, for such a religious family, you guys sure missed a lot of churches yesterday." Scott leaned against Rachel's locker before homeroom, garnering her a few appraising looks from boys who never looked at her before and a few glares from the upper-crust girls who were obviously confused why Scott would be talking to her. *Let 'em stare*, Rachel thought. *Let's give 'em something to stare at.* With a brazenness that she'd never felt in all her sixteen years, Rachel walked up to Scott, put an arm behind his head, and pulled his mouth to hers.

He stiffened for a moment, as if unsure how to react to her actions, then he put an arm around her waist and pressed her hard against the lockers. She felt the hard muscles of his chest press into her, and her hand traced down his neck to his broad shoulders. He returned her kiss with a fire she'd never felt, and something inside her broke loose in a silent exultation, like a powerful beast that had lain dormant for far too long.

Rachel recognized the feeling; it was the same thrill she'd felt in her dreams when she was flying, chasing the other dragon, capturing, joining, becoming one with her—

"Whoa, tiger!" Rachel broke the kiss with a gasp, looking up into Scott's wide eyes.

"Yeah, definitely whoa." A bead of sweat stood out on his temple and rolled down the side of his face. Rachel barely resisted the urge to lean in and lick it up. *Where did* that *come from?*

"Yes. Definitely whoa." A new voice broke the pair apart as they turned to meet the icy glare of Delmount Sturgis, head of the math department and legendary extinguisher of "hall hanky-panky" as he called it. Mr. Sturgis had been known to sneak up behind particularly involved couples at school dances and pour large cups of ice water on the amorous teens.

Rachel and Scott looked at Mr. Sturgis, then looked at each other, then back to the diminutive bald man, who was almost shaking in his righteous fury at having his hallways defiled with more rampant teenage hormones. Rachel broke first, collapsing into giggles and turning to run toward her homeroom. Scott followed suit, and moments later, they were seated safely across the aisle from each other in Mrs. Hicklin's homeroom class.

"What brought that on?" Scott asked. "Not that I'm complaining, of course, but wasn't that a little, um, much for an early morning hello?"

"Yeah, uh, about that…Look, I didn't mean for all that to happen. I mean, I meant to kiss you, but not *kiss you* kiss you, you know what I mean? I meant a little 'hi there, back off girls' kinda kiss, not a…"

"Not a 'hi, honey, glad you made it home from the wars now take me right now' kinda kiss?"

"Yeah, not that. So, um, sorry?" Rachel couldn't look at Scott while they held their whispered conversation, so she spent the whole time staring at her shoes and wishing that her life in hiking boots and bike shoes let her paint her toenails like other girls, but then she thought that if she was like other girls, maybe Scott wouldn't like her after all, and then she thought he'd been quiet a really long time, so she finally looked up at him. "Sorry, did you say something?"

"Yeah." Scott's hair was messy, and some of it hung down over one eye in a way that made Rachel really *really* want to reach out and fix it, but she held off because, well, homeroom and all.

"Well, what did you say?"

"I said I'm not." Scott gave her one of those little lopsided grins that flashed just enough teeth and made the dimple on his right cheek show itself and generally made her knees weak.

"You're not what?" Rachel asked, pretty sure she'd missed more than one something at this point.

"I'm not sorry. Whatever made you kiss me like that, I hope it happens more often. Because it was amazing. You're pretty amazing, Rachel Hampton."

Rachel was about to say something that probably just would have made her feel even more stupid, but the bell for first period rang and saved her. She had first period English, and Scott had first period Chem, so their next chance to talk would be lunch.

"See ya," Rachel said as she gathered her book bag and headed for the door before she could do something else to embarrass herself. *Now where did that kiss come from? Not that I didn't like it, but it didn't feel like it all came from me.*

It may not have, youngling, came a voice in her head that Rachel knew for a fact wasn't herself or one of the normal voices every teenager hears.

Who the hell is this?

I believe that our bond may be deeper than I first imagined, said the voice, and Rachel suddenly knew exactly who was in her head.

Auros?

Yes, it is I.

How did you get in my head?

I believe when I healed you, I may have imbued you with more of my essence than we originally thought. Then our proximity last night and the excitement of battle and pursuit has led to deeper intermingling of our thoughts. I will attempt to separate myself as soon as possible, my apologies.

Wait! This might be good. What if those guys come to get you? If I know immediately, I can maybe help. And isn't this what made me able to find you yesterday?

Yes, but to bond at this level with a dragon can be...uncomfortable for some humans. And I may find myself intruding on your private thoughts.

Some of those private thoughts, and dreams, from the night before bubbled to the surface right then, and Rachel blushed, looked around, and realized with a start that she was standing stock-still in an almost deserted hallway. She bolted to English class, but not before shooting a final thought at Auros. *Just keep out of my mental underwear drawer, and we'll be fine. We need to keep tabs on you for now. Once you're somewhere safe and Bentley has been dealt with, we'll figure out how to un-bond.*

As you wish.

~

"So there's a dragon in your head, and that's why you kissed me like that?" Scott didn't look up from the napkin he was blotting his pizza with. He slowly took the grease-sodden paper and set it off to one side of his lunch tray.

"Well, Auros isn't the only reason I kissed you like that," Rachel said, concentrating intently on removing the crusts from the turkey and bacon sandwich her dad made her for lunch. The two sat at the far end of a long row of lunch tables, a white Formica ocean of teen angst and horrible nutrition, separated from their classmates by their book bags piled on the tables to make a barricade against joiners.

Rachel peeked up at Scott, her cheeks blazing red, only to catch him peeking up at her at the same time. They both laughed, and the tension was broken. "God, look at us," Scott said. "We spent practically every waking moment of Saturday together, and now we're apart for like one day, and it's like everything's different."

"We're idiots," Rachel said, reaching across the table for his hand.

"Careful, pizza grease." Scott pulled his hand below the table, wiped it on his jeans, and then took hers. "All better."

"You're a Neanderthal. Wiping pizza grease on your pants! What would your mother say?"

"Probably that I shouldn't listen to any girl from this dump of a town, no matter how much she agrees with you."

"Oh, so Mrs. Morrison isn't a fan of our little burg?"

"You could say that. You could also say that she reminds my dad of it every day and night, at top volume. But you don't need to hear about my ridiculous home life; you've got your own issues."

"Not the least of which is a dragon hanging out in my head. Speaking of which, hang on a minute." *Auros, are you there? Are you hearing this?*

Yes, I am listening. And you human children are very amusing with your courtship rituals. Why do you not just mate as you wish?

Rachel's cheeks went hot again, and Scott raised an eyebrow. Just then, someone cleared his throat beside Rachel, and a voice said, "Private party? Or can anyone join?"

Rachel looked up at Billy standing there holding his lunch tray and moved her book bag onto the floor. Billy set his tray on the table next to hers and started unpacking his lunch. "So, what's going on? Are we making plans to get the d-r-a-g-o-n to safety?"

"Billy, you know everyone around here can spell dragon, right?" Rachel smacked Billy's hand as he snagged a scrap of bacon.

"Ow! Yes, Miss Literal, I know everybody can spell dragon. I was just being funny. Damn, life's tough for the young, misunderstood comedian."

"Or the young, completely understood jackass," Rachel shot back.

"Ouch," Billy repeated. "So what's new on the scaly front?"

"Rachel's got dragon ESP to go with her GPS," Scott said.

"What?"

"Auros is in her head, dude. The dragon can talk to her, even here."

Billy turned to Rachel. "Is this for real? The dragon talks to you? Are you sure you're not nuts?"

"No, I'm not sure I'm not nuts, but yes, Auros can talk to me telepathically. He thinks that when he healed me, we were linked somehow, and when I was exposed to his magic the other night, it deepened the bond. So now we can communicate mentally."

"That's cool," Billy said. "So what's the plan? We gonna ride the dragon to the black helicopter dudes' headquarters and have him breathe fire all over their sorry asses? Or is he just gonna magic them all into zombies or turn them into frogs or something?"

Tell your friend that humans do not ride dragons into battle like flying horses, and I don't use my flame lightly. And ask him to please chew with his mouth closed. He is disgusting.

Rachel relayed the message, giggling as she watched Billy's mouth snap shut, then continued. "I don't know what the plan is. For now, we've got to convince my dad that Auros isn't evil, that Bentley is the bad guy, and that he has to stop Scott's dad from re-opening the mine tomorrow."

"What do I do? Drive the getaway car? Raid the armory? Operate the bat-signal?" Billy was almost bouncing on his plastic lunchroom chair in excitement.

"For now, you hang loose and let us work our angles," Scott said. "I'll go to my father and try to get him to hold off opening the mine again for another couple of days, out of respect. I'll tell him that he should at least leave it closed a week in honor of the men who died. If he does that, I think we can figure everything out by Friday."

"And I'll try to convince my dad not to go out dragon-hunting, and maybe, just maybe, set up a face-to-face with him and a certain golden-scaled fire breather so that Auros can apologize and explain his actions."

I am not accustomed to explaining my actions to lesser species.

And that's part of the problem, pal. You can't keep thinking of humans as a lesser species. It's our world now, has been for a long time. And if you want to keep living in it, you're going to have to behave. Otherwise, humans will end up hunting you to extinction.

I understand this. It is simply that old habits take time to change. I will...try.

"So what do I do, just sit at home twiddling my thumbs?" Billy asked.

"For right now, yes. There's nothing you can do right now, and we need to be careful how we approach this whole thing. So sit at home and twiddle your thumbs, and when we need somebody to drive the getaway car, you're the man." Rachel smiled at him, but Billy picked up his lunch tray and walked off.

"What's up?" Rachel said, following him.

"What's up? What are you, kidding? I've been your best friend since you got here, and now that Richie Rich is paying you a little bit of attention, I'm just supposed to wait around for you to remember me? What the hell, Rachel? He's just some rich asshole. What do you even see in him?"

"He's nice, Billy, which is more than I can say for how you've been acting the past couple of days. He's not the one who made a huge scene at the Sandbar. That was you, remember?"

"Yeah, I remember. I remember all the other girls he's brought to the Sandbar all year, too."

"What are you saying?" Rachel's eyebrows came together, and she looked up at her best friend.

"I'm saying that I don't want to see you get hurt, Rachel. And he's going to hurt you. It might not be today, it might not be tomorrow, but eventually if you mess around with guys like Scott, you're gonna get hurt. And I just hope you've still got some real friends around when that happens." Billy tossed his tray on the conveyor belt and slammed open the lunchroom doors. Rachel stood just inside, watching him stomp down the hill toward his truck.

"What's that about?" Scott's voice came over her shoulder. "I didn't want to get too close, seemed like I might be part of the problem."

"Yeah, Billy's gone all green-eyed monster again. I wish he understood that I just don't see him that way."

"It's tough, getting friend-zoned from the hottest girl in school."

"Who? Me? The hottest girl in school?" She turned around to see Scott smiling down at her.

"Don't sweat Billy. He'll come around."

"I just hope he doesn't do anything stupid before then."

CHAPTER 21

"So what was it like, way back in the day? Were there no people, or just not many, or what? Did the elves live in houses, or in trees, or houses in the trees? C'mon, tell me a story!" Rachel wheedled. She was sitting with her back to a huge oak tree by the quarry where Auros had been hiding all day. Scott lay on his back with his head on her legs as a pillow, looking up at the clear sky through the canopy of thick leaves and branches.

"There were humans, but not many. Your race had not yet bred the rest of the world into submission," Auros said with a chuckle. "Elves were never a plentiful race, but they were long-lived and strong in magic, so they controlled much of the world's forests and traveled freely across the seas between continents. We dragons kept mainly to the mountains, coming down now and again to study magic alongside the elven masters, or to hunt."

"Are you immortal? I mean, how did you stay alive for so long under the mountain?" Scott asked.

"We can be killed, as can the elves, but we will not die of old age. When it is time for a dragon to pass into the flames, he or she usually flies off over the horizon to live out the rest of his days in solitude. But truth be told, I doubt one could find much solitude today with the way you little apelings have covered every corner of the world."

"There's always the North Pole, big guy," Scott replied.

"I do not like the cold. I prefer it down here where it is warm and I can fly on the warm winds." Auros glared at the boy.

"Can we fly again? This time without the panic?" Rachel asked.

"I thought I was to stay out of sight. I would not want to cause trouble for you." Auros raised an eyebrow at the girl, and Rachel realized he was teasing.

She punched the tawny-haired dragon-boy in the shoulder and mock-growled at him. "Change, scaly-dude, or I'll have to turn you over to the elves."

Auros laughed at her fake ferocity, and the air around him shimmered. Where a teenaged boy had sat, now a huge golden dragon stood. Auros stretched his wings and rolled his head from side to side in an eerily human stretch. Rachel reached for his wing, then froze as a branch snapped behind them.

"Rachel, get away from the monster." Her father's voice came from the trees.

Rachel stepped back from Auros' side and turned to see her father, Mr. Bentley, and three men in black combat uniforms step out of the woods. The three men held machine guns pointed at Auros, and Bentley had a small black pistol held down by his side.

"Dad! What are you doing here? How did you find us?" Rachel asked, moving between the gunmen and the dragon.

"Your friend Billy came to me this afternoon and told me you were off in the woods with this creature and that Morrison boy. He was worried about you. Looks like he had good reason to be."

"Auros is no threat to anybody. He's our friend," Rachel protested.

"He attacked me and killed Ed," her father replied.

"We'll take care of the beast, Mr. Hampton. You just take your daughter and her little friend and get them clear of the danger." Bentley stepped forward, raising his gun and pointing it at the dragon's head. "We don't want any more humans to be harmed, do we, dragon?"

"I would prefer if you would address me by my name, Silvaren. And yes, I know exactly who and what you are. I can smell it on you like the stench of betrayal. I am Auros, son of Ebon and Goldwing, and you will show me the respect due one of my kind." Auros shifted back to his human form, but instead of the jeans and t-shirt he had been wearing, now he was clad in gleaming chain mail with a solid golden breastplate bearing an image of a dragon in flight on his chest. A winged helmet sat on his head, his eyes barely visible through the slit of his visor. In one hand, he held a wicked-looking curved sword, and in the other a round shield, also gleaming gold in the afternoon sunlight.

"Fine, then, Auros. You must come with us where you will be safe," Bentley said, adjusting his aim to the now-human-sized dragon's face.

"I am safe here. You are the only one threatening me. These humans you brought present no danger."

Rachel gasped as Auros flashed into motion. Quicker than her eye could follow, the dragon-boy lashed out with his sword and cut through the guns held by the two closest soldiers. The third man found himself suddenly standing face-to-face with a fully armored vision of medieval threat and raised his rifle to his shoulder, only to have it snatched away and the barrel bent perpendicular to the stock.

"I believe I mentioned that I am in no danger from these men," Auros repeated, turning his attention back to Bentley. Rachel noticed that through all of Auros' movements, Bentley managed to track the dragon with his pistol effortlessly.

"No, but you are a danger to them," the suited man said. Bentley holstered his gun and held up both hands to Auros. "You killed a man at the mine. That cannot go unanswered."

"I apologize for that misunderstanding. He threatened me, and I overreacted. It will not happen again. I most humbly offer my condolences and will pay whatever recompense his family desires." Auros inclined his head to Ben in apology.

"Nobody wants money for this, um, Auros. I just want to know that my daughter is safe. And you can understand how nothing about your little display just now is very reassuring," Ben replied, stepping in front of Rachel.

"Dad, Auros is my friend. He wouldn't hurt me. He even got between Billy and Scott when they were being stupid and knocked me over at the Sandbar," Rachel said.

"It matters not. You are coming with me, dragon, and that is final," Bentley said, raising his pistol again.

"What makes you think that pea-shooter is going to have any more luck than your boys there?" Scott asked with a lopsided grin. "After all, if he doesn't sweat assault rifles, why should he sweat a Glock?"

Bentley turned to face Rachel, his gun hand tracking until the barrel pointed at the girl's face. "Because he can't outrun a bullet, and while it might not hurt him, it will kill this idiot girl. Now put these on and come with me." He tossed a pair of familiar manacles at Auros, who caught them and stared at Bentley.

"You would harm an innocent?" the dragon asked.

"What the hell is this?" Ben asked, trying to step between his daughter and the coldly smiling Bentley.

"Back up, Hampton, or I'll put a round in your daughter's face. Auros, put the manacles on. The cold iron will keep you in your human form until I get you back to the mine. And the rest of you, get down and put your noses on the ground. If you move before I'm gone with the dragon, I'll shoot the girl." Bentley kept the gun steady on Rachel, smiling all the while.

"Don't I get a vote?" Rachel asked.

"What? No, shut up!" Bentley replied, stepping forward so his pistol was just inches away from her face.

"Not gonna happen," the girl said with a snarl. "I just hope this is as easy as it looks on TV," she said, smacking the gun aside and aiming a kick at the juncture of the tall man's legs. The gun went off, deafening her, and Auros tossed the manacles to the ground and dove at Bentley.

Bentley ducked to one side as the dragon-boy flew at him, and Auros crashed to the ground several feet from him. The air around Bentley shimmered with a reddish light, and where once a nonde-script man in a black suit and sunglasses stood, a nearly seven-foot-tall armored warrior with angular features, long jet-black hair, and pointed ears remained.

"Holy shit, he really is an elf," Scott murmured from where he knelt on the forest floor.

"I am indeed, human, and you are dead." Bentley waved his hand, and a sword appeared. He swung at Scott's throat, but Rachel reached down and pulled him back as the blade whistled through empty air.

"Your quarrel is not with them, Bentley. It's me you want, so come and get me." Auros regained his feet and charged the elf with his sword raised high. The dragon and elf battled all over the clearing, moving faster than the human eye could follow. Ben, Scott, and Rachel ducked behind trees to stay out of the fray as the soldiers got to their feet and ran off.

After several long minutes of blurred fighting, Bentley stopped in the center of the clearing and held his hands high above his head. A glowing ball of red light coalesced around his outstretched hands, and he hurled the orb of energy at the hiding humans. Auros flickered into view directly in the path of the energy-ball and deflected it into the sky with his shield. He crashed into the trunk of the tree from the force of the blow as the energy-ball flew into the sky and exploded like a Fourth of July fireworks finale.

Bentley conjured his sword again and charged Auros, but Rachel shoved the dragon out of the way at the last possible second. Bentley's sword pierced the girl just below her ribcage, pinning her to the tree. Rachel's mouth opened in a soundless "O" of pain, and Auros screamed in shared agony.

The elf yanked his sword free and turned to the dragon-boy. "You've bonded with her. Well, that's convenient. While you feel her pain, I can just finish this." He raised his sword, but before he could deliver the killing blow, five loud *cracks* filled the clearing.

Bentley sagged to one knee as Scott kept the elf's own discarded pistol trained on him. "You should run now, you son of a bitch. Because if we can't heal her, I don't know what I might do." The elf did just that, *blurring* out of sight. Scott sagged back against the tree, gun hanging loose in his hand.

Ben and Auros were already at Rachel's side, Ben stroking her hair and Auros trying to get at the wound. The dragon laid his hands upon the gash in her belly and closed his eyes. A golden glow surrounded him, flowing from his head and shoulders down his arms to his hands, then out to Rachel's still form. The dragon laid hands on the girl for several moments; then his shoulders sagged, and he fell forward across Rachel's body.

"Is she?" Ben asked.

"She will be fine. She will recover. But I must rest," the dragon said, breathless.

Rachel's eyes fluttered open, and she looked up at her father and the dragon laying asleep on her chest. "Ouch," she said, then turned her head to the side and fell fast asleep.

"Ouch indeed," Ben said, sitting back on his heels.

"Yeah," Scott agreed, sitting on the ground beside him. "Now how are we going to get them out of here?"

CHAPTER 22

Auros recovered first and made it out of the forest to Scott's truck under his own power. Scott and Ben helped a woozy but conscious Rachel get into Ben's SUV, and they drove to the Hampton home. Rachel waved off any help getting out of the car but allowed her father to take her arm and help her up the stairs onto the porch.

"You boys might as well come in. We need to figure out what to do next, and I need to figure out how I'm going to apologize to my daughter," Ben said as he opened the front door and stepped into the house.

Scott and Auros followed close behind Ben and Rachel, almost bumping into Ben's broad back as he stopped cold in the foyer. Billy sat on the couch in the den, his knee jiggling as he looked at the returning group.

"Before you say anything, let me talk," Billy said, bouncing to his feet. "I know what I did was stupid, and I'm really, really sorry. After the whole thing at lunch today, I lost my head, and I called Mr. Hampton and told him Rachel was hanging out with the dragon in the woods, and that he should call that Bentley guy and take care of him. It was stupid, I'm an asshole, and I'm really, really sorry. And I understand if you never want to see me again, Rachel. But I gotta say this. I love you. I've loved you since the minute I laid eyes on you, and to see you with this rich douchebag was just more than I could handle. So, I'm sorry, and if you want me to leave, just say so. What I did was wrong, and I regret that, but I'm never going to regret being in love with you."

He stood in the center of the den, staring at Rachel and her father with a clenched jaw and gleaming eyes. Rachel gently pried her father's hand from her arm and took a few shaky steps into the room to stand in front of Billy.

"You were nice to me when nobody else here was. You've been my best friend since day one, Billy. But that's all we've ever been—friends. I don't know where this crazy idea that we were going to be something more came from, and I don't care. You almost got Auros kidnapped today, and you almost got me *killed*. So yeah, I don't ever want to see you again. Now get out of my house, and stay out of my life."

"But Rachel—" Billy reached for her arm, and Rachel slapped him across the cheek. His face snapped to one side, and Rachel watched as the muscles in his neck clenched.

He turned back to her and said, "Fine, you want the rich kid and the overgrown lizard, you can have them. Just remember who your real friends are when they're done with you. Oh wait, you won't have any left. Never mind." He shouldered past Auros and Scott and slammed through the screen door onto the porch.

Silence hung in the room for a long moment as Ben and the boys looked everywhere but at Rachel. Rachel looked from Scott, to Auros, to her father, then back to the dragon, then back to Scott, then heaved a sigh and sat down on the couch. "Well, that was awkward. Now can we get back to planning insurrection and devastation of the evil elf cabal that wants to wake up a herd of dragons and destroy humanity as we know it? I'm thirsty, and I've been stabbed, so I think I get a day off from playing serving wench. Dad, there's some sodas and beer in the fridge. Would you grab three Pepsis and whatever you want?"

"Yes, sweetie." Ben walked past his daughter to the kitchen, laying a gentle hand on her shoulder as he passed. Rachel reached up to quickly squeeze her father's hand and gave him a slight smile. Scott looked from chair to couch and back again before Rachel patted the sofa cushion next to her. He grinned like a little boy on Christmas morning and sat next to her.

"Where should I sit?" Auros asked. "There seems to be some importance placed on these things, and as I am unaccustomed to human dwellings, I do not understand the significance."

"Sit here, bro." Scott patted the other cushion on the couch, putting Auros on the other side of him. "One rule of 'human dwellings' is that you never sit in another dude's recliner." He pointed to the brown leather chair that held pride of place in front of the television. "That's like the throne in a castle. You sit in a man's chair, it's the next best thing to an invasion."

"Thank you. That is good to know," Auros replied. Rachel covered her mouth to hide a smile as her father brought the drinks in from the kitchen.

"Okay," Ben began after everyone was situated with beverage and seated. "So, what is this Mr. Bentley, and what does he want with Auros? And why are you so hell-bent on stopping him?"

"Bentley is an elven mage, hiding within human society for millennia," Auros answered. "He wishes to awaken the dragons and use my people to once again subjugate humans under the rule of the elves and dragons. But I fear that he would not stop there. I believe from his actions that he would not be satisfied sharing power, and once the humans were put in their place, he would destroy the dragons and rule alone."

"Elven...mage? Dragons?" Ben took a long pull from his beer and stood up. He disappeared into the kitchen and came back with a six-pack of Yeungling bottles. He finished his first and twisted the top off a second, knocking back half of it in one long swallow. "Sorry. I might need a little higher degree of mental lubrication for this conversation."

"I understand," Auros replied. "There seem to be many things that humans have forgotten or relegated to legend since we have slumbered. But it is crucial that you believe what I say. The fate of your world may depend on it."

"Well, Auros, if you have come to me a week ago with this story, I'd be calling for people to take you to a nice room with padded walls. But since then, I've seen you in all your glory, and I've seen Bentley turn from a harmless bureaucrat into some pointy-eared ninja. So I'm pretty inclined to believe a lot of things. But how do we stop Bentley? Is he acting alone? Is this some kind of conspiracy?"

"That's what we need you to figure out, Dad. We're kids, so nobody will give us the time of day. But you can get things done that we can't. We need your help."

"I can try, but there are plenty of people that won't give me the time of day, either. What do I need to do?"

"Well, the biggest thing is to keep my father from re-opening the mine. Auros says that will wake up the rest of the dragons, and that's probably not going to be good for anybody," Scott said.

"I can probably keep the mine closed for another day or two, but there's no way I can get it closed permanently. Is there anything we can do to keep the dragons from waking up?" Ben asked Auros.

"If the sleeping chamber is breached, the dragons will awaken, just as I did. But perhaps we can change the direction of your tunnel to prevent that from happening. The shaft that you dug into my chamber was relatively small. It should be a simple matter to alter the course of the digging," Auros replied.

"Yeah, not so much. Tell him about the great plan you guys are working on up there on the mountain, Dad," Rachel said, giving her father a wry look.

"The process is called mountaintop removal mining. The shaft that woke you was a small shaft that we plan to use to plant explosives in the mountaintop to, well, it's kind of hard to explain…" Ben trailed off as Auros' eyes grew wide.

"They're going to drop tons of explosives down the shaft and blow the whole top off the mountain. Not exactly a subtle wakeup for a bunch of sleeping dragons, huh?" Rachel cut in as her father looked on.

"That...that sounds terrible," Auros said. "That would certainly bring to the surface a host of terrified and angry dragons, bent on the destruction of whoever or whatever disturbed their rest. They would wake up thinking they were under attack and would destroy anyone in the vicinity. This must have been part of Bentley's plan all along, to create a violent awakening so there could be no chance for a peaceful meeting between human and dragon."

"Wait a minute, Auros," Ben interrupted. "Before we get all nuts with the conspiracy theories, remember that Bentley has nothing to do with the mining operation."

"Yeah," Scott chimed in. "My dad bought the land years ago and has been mining in this area for decades. As a matter of fact, our family has mined around here all the way back for centuries."

"That explains it!" Auros exclaimed. "You're an elf! I wondered why you didn't smell like the other humans. You're part elven. Your family must be part of the plan with Bentley."

"Dude, I'm not an elf. I don't have pointy ears, and I don't even really like trees and stuff," Scott protested, but one hand crept up to feel his ears, almost as of its own volition.

"It's the only explanation," Auros argued. "Your father was probably all of the miners for all the generations. He just pretended to grow old and die every so often to keep the humans from being suspicious."

"Didn't you say when we did that history project about genealogy that you never knew your grandfather?" Rachel added. She reached out and patted Scott's knee. He took her hand in his and held it tight.

"That's because he died before I was born. He died, Rachel. I've been to his grave. And what about my mom? She's totally human, right down to her temper. If my dad had some kind of elven magic, don't you think he'd make her be nicer to him?"

"I would have if I could, son, but magic has its limits." A new voice came from the doorway. Rachel turned and stood as Scott's father, Gerald Morrison, stepped into the room. He held a small black pistol aimed at Auros.

The dragon stood and smiled at him. "You know that won't hurt me." He nodded at the gun.

"I know," Morrison said, moving the gun to Rachel. "But if I kill her, it won't do much for you, will it? You're bonded, dragon. That means that if I kill her, you'll die, too. And you're very quickly climbing the list of creatures I want to see dead."

"Dad, what the hell? What are you doing here? With a gun? Tell them this whole elf thing is crazy and then let's figure out how not to wake up the dragons!" Scott stepped in front of Rachel, using his body as a shield.

"I'm afraid I can't do that, son." The air around Morrison shimmered, and where a normal man in khakis and a polo shirt stood seconds before, a seven-foot tall elf with long brown hair, razor-sharp features, and deep green eyes stood in brown leather armor. He still held the pistol, but the hilt of a sword stuck out over one shoulder. His ears were lobeless and swept up into very pronounced points.

"Sorry, Scott. They're right. I'm a little better than a normal human. Actually, I'm a *lot* better than a human. I am Varen of the elven, one of the rightful rulers of this world, and we will no longer stand by and let these hairless apes take over on the basis of their capacity to breed rapidly. Come with me, dragon, and no one needs to get hurt. Well, actually, you do, but come along anyway, and I won't kill the girl. You too, Scott. I need you for this part."

"What part?" Rachel asked. "And they aren't going anywhere."

"Oh, they are," Morrison said. "And I don't think this is the part where I give you the whole monologue. This is the part where I tell my son and the dragon to put these on and go sit in the bed of my pickup. Or I'll kill your father, then you." Morrison pulled two pair of dull gray handcuffs from his belt and tossed one to Auros and one to Scott.

"Cold iron," Auros hissed as he clapped the handcuffs around his wrists.

"That's right, o' scaled one. Saps the power right out of you, doesn't it? You can't cast spells, can't change form, can't even use your full strength, can you?" Morrison smiled as Auros and Scott filed out past him to the waiting truck. Rachel rushed to the door as he went down their porch steps and headed to the pickup. Morrison paused just long enough to fire a round into the front tires of her father's SUV and the engine block before getting in the driver's seat and leaving with his captives.

CHAPTER 23

"Hurry up!" Rachel stood tapping her foot as her father crawled out from under the front of his SUV.

"There's no point in hurrying, dear. That bastard Morrison put a slug straight through my radiator and flywheel. This poor girl isn't going anywhere until she sees the inside of a garage for some surgery." Ben stood and brushed off his jeans. "Let me call the police."

"There's no point, Dad. They've got to be in on it. He's got a whole secret arm of the government, complete with black helicopters. I doubt Sheriff Spencer and his bunch of Deputy Dawgs is going to be able to do anything. They can't even keep kids from sneaking booze into high school football games!" She turned and stomped around the corner of the house.

Her father's voice hung in the air after her. "Where are you going?"

"To fix this." Rachel came back around the house walking her bike and carrying her helmet. "I'm going up to the mine. I can get through security without anyone seeing me, and maybe I can stop Scott's father before he does anything stupid."

"There is no way in hell you're going up there alone. That psycho will shoot you!" Ben stepped in front of her, but Rachel held up a hand glowing red. Ben stared, mouth hanging open as his daughter's hand burst into flame.

"Not if I shoot him first, Dad. Remember when I told you Auros healed me and now we're bonded? Well, he's in my head now, and I can feel what he's feeling. He's terrified of what Mr. Morrison is going to do, and not just for himself. He knows how bad it will be for all of humanity if the dragons come back, so he's been teaching me how to use his powers. I can handle myself a lot better than you think."

"I still don't want you to go."

"And I don't want Scott and Auros to die. And I don't want a whole bunch of dragons to wake up pissed off and hungry. And I don't want the whole world to end because I stayed home like a scared little girl. Now get out of my way. If you can get the truck fixed, follow me. If not, call ahead to the mine and tell the guards to keep Mr. Morrison out. Tell them he's gone crazy or something." With that, she threw one leg over the bike's seat and pushed off. In seconds, she was racing through the woods, climbing fast as she bounced over familiar trails toward the mine and what just might be the end of the world.

Rachel made the half-hour ride to the mine in twenty minutes, but it was clear as soon as she got near the front gates that Morrison had beat her there. The gate stood open, and the guard house looked unattended from a distance. As Rachel got closer, she saw a hole in one window and a splatter of blood on the opposite wall that told her Larry the gate guard had gotten her father's call and tried to stop the elf, but got a bullet for his troubles.

She dropped the bike beside the guard shack and continued up the hill on foot, trying to keep out of sight as best she could. It wasn't easy in the basically wide-open surroundings of a working coal mine, but she darted from rock outcropping to truck to road grader and tried to use the scattered heavy equipment as cover.

She reached the huge hole in the side of the mountain where Auros had sprung from his slumber just four days before and thought,

Was that really just a few days ago? It seems like the whole world has changed in less than a week. She dropped to her belly and crawled the last few feet to the edge of the hole and peered in. Morrison stood in the bottom of the crater, fully restored to his elven form with his sword in his hand. Auros and Scott knelt before him, hands shackled behind their backs.

"Now, by the shedding of the blood of the three races of Earth, the spell of slumber will be broken. By the power of the old gods, I present these offerings to bring the lost race back from the darkness and take their rightful place of dominion over these insipid humans."

"Aren't you missing a race, Dad? I get that I'm your human sacrifice, and Auros is the dragon, but don't you need an elf, too?" Scott spit blood at his father's feet and grinned up at the elf.

"You're not human, son, no matter how much it pains me to call you that. You are a mongrel, a disgusting mix of human and elf that the world will be well rid of. That's why the cold iron burns your arms, boy. Your mother was human, but I am full elven, so your blood will suffice for two races."

"As much as I appreciate the economy of using Scott to fill two categories, I'd rather you not slice up my boyfriend. So why don't you toss me the key to those handcuffs and I won't burn you to a cinder where you stand," Rachel said, standing up and striding down the sloped side of the crater. She spoke forcefully, almost shouting across the distance, all the while thinking, *please don't let my knees shake so bad that I fall down.*

Somehow she made it down the pile of loose rock and dirt and stood across the crater from Morrison, almost completely steady. She raised her right hand and wrapped it in flame. "I think I said let them go."

"I think you also threatened to burn me where I stood. Well, now I'm standing here, so what are you going to do about it?" Morrison sneered from where he stood suddenly just inches from her nose.

He is fast, but you are just as fast. Trust your abilities. Auros' voice in her head was faint and distorted, like it was coming from a great distance.

Is that the cold iron?

Yes, it interferes with our bond. I would not be able to speak with you at all were you any farther away.

Then I'll try to stay close. I might need all the coaching I can get. Rachel offered up a silent prayer to a God she believed in a lot more than she had a week ago and swung a flaming fist at Morrison's head. He easily dodged to one side, but his eyes bulged and his face went pale when Rachel's knee swung up and caught him squarely in the crotch. The elf dropped to his knees, and Rachel caught him right in the nose with a looping uppercut. Morrison sprawled on his back in the dirt, his eyes rolled back in his head.

Rachel stood over the fallen elf for a few seconds, staring with wide eyes at the first person she'd ever punched. "Well, that went better than I expected," she said, then knelt by Morrison's unconscious form and patted his front pockets. She pulled a fat ring of keys from his pocket and went over to where Auros and Scott were shackled. Seconds later, the boys were free, and the three started up the side of the crater to make their escape.

Their progress was cut off when Bentley appeared over the lip of hole holding a very large pistol and pulling Rachel's father along beside him. "I thought you were likely to be a problem, so when Varen called and told me to meet him here, I decided to bring along a little insurance. Looks like a good idea."

"Very good, Silvaren," Morrison/Varen said from where he had struggled to his feet.

Can you get to my father before Bentley shoots him? Rachel thought at Auros.

If I can get some type of distraction.

I've got distraction covered. You just save my dad, Rachel replied silently, then whirled to face Morrison. She clapped her hands together in front of her, concentrating on the concept of fire. Flames leapt from her fingertips in a steady line of white-hot fire aimed straight for Morrison. The elf danced out of the way, but Rachel kept sending bolt after bolt of flame at him, forcing him to leap from side to side to keep from being burnt to a cinder. She felt more than heard

Auros bolt from her side to rescue her father, but the sound of Bentley/Silvaren gasping in pain was one she found pleasantly familiar.

Morrison could mount no kind of offense as he skipped out of the way of the flames, and after a few moments of jumping around, his footing betrayed him on the loose stone, and he sprawled on his knees, looking up at the furious teen.

"Let's see how you like it when somebody else is throwing magic around, asshole," Rachel muttered and drew a bead on the elf's face. She let fly with a final bolt of flame, but Scott reached out and knocked her arm off target just as she fired.

"What the hell, Scott?" She turned to face him, trying to extinguish her fingertips so she didn't accidentally catch her boyfriend on fire.

"I can't let you cook my dad, Rache." He wouldn't look her in the eye, like he was embarrassed to help his father.

"He was going to kill you to open up a portal to bring back the dragons and destroy the world! He called you a mongrel! He's the bad guy, Scott!"

"But he's still my father. And if we kill him, are we any better than he is?"

"You've been reading too many old *X-Men* comics. He'll murder us both if we give him half a chance."

"She's right, you know." Morrison suddenly appeared behind his son, sword in hand. He gave Rachel an evil grin and ran Scott through. The boy collapsed onto Rachel, his mouth gasping open and his eyes filling up with tears as Morrison pulled four feet of steel back out of his chest.

"Bentley!" the elf cried up the hill. "Finish off that overgrown lizard and bring me his body. He doesn't have to be very alive for the ceremony to work, so cut off anything you don't need."

"A little easier said than done, sir!" Bentley shouted back, throwing himself into a standing backflip to get out of range of Auros' conjured sword.

Rachel watched in horror as Morrison stepped past Scott and smashed a fist into the side of her face. She tried to roll with the punch but still went down like she'd been hit with a brick. She collapsed to the ground, head spinning, and watched as Morrison knelt down, tossed his son's body over one shoulder like a sack of potatoes, and turned to go back to the crater.

Rachel tried to get to her feet, but dizziness claimed her before she even made it to her knees. She shook her head to clear her vision and immediately regretted it as a wave of nausea crashed over her. She watched with blurred vision as Morrison set Scott down on the ground and began to wave his arms in a complex series of hand motions. Behind him, a glowing portal began to shimmer into being in the sand. A rainbow of colors oscillated through the opening—red, blue, silver, gold, green, orange, purple, black, white—everything imaginable. The portal grew and grew until it was nearly thirty feet across, and the images became more distinct as Morrison's intricate motions flew faster and faster.

"You need elf, human, and dragon blood to open the portal, Varen! I think you shall find yourself short on dragon blood because I intend mine to remain right where it is!" Auros bellowed from the top of the crater. Rachel turned to focus on his fight and watched as Bentley scored a deep slash along Auros' side, cutting through his armor and the flesh beneath. Rachel's eyes widened, then she let out a little laugh as she realized the feint the dragon had pulled off. By letting the elf score a painful but harmless cut on him, he got Bentley/Silvaren within his reach, dropped his sword, and twisted the elf's neck until a sharp *snap* echoed across the mine.

"I can open the portal with a drop of your blood, fool, and you've spilled more than enough for me to work with." Morrison grinned as Bentley's bloody sword floated into the air and flew across the crater to him. Morrison stopped his casting long enough to turn and plunge the sword into the portal. The second the dragon blood touched the milky gateway, the images coalesced into a mass of dragons in all colors, all trapped, all desperate to get out, all very, very angry.

"Now I throw this worthless mutt through the opening, and the dragons will be released from the magical dimension where they've been trapped for all the years." Morrison stopped his hand-waving and knelt to pick up Scott's body. Rachel could see him wince when his father grabbed him, so she knew he was still alive. For the moment, at least.

"What do you mean, magical dimension? The other dragons have slumbered beneath the earth, as I did," Auros said, running down to block Morrison from getting Scott to the portal.

"You foolish child! Do you really think your race would agree to go to sleep for thousands of years? No, idiot, they are all awake, just tucked away in a magical dimension that can only be reached through a sacrifice of human, elf, and dragon. Your uncle stuck you in the dirt with your stupid plan to 'warn the humans' because he knew you loved the little hairless apes. You were never supposed to wake up, idiot. You were the only dragon interested in saving humanity. The rest just wanted to leave the world long enough for humanity to learn how to behave or destroy itself. Well, these monkeys will obviously never learn to behave, and they're taking too damned long to destroy themselves, so now I'll bring back the dragons, and we'll burn them into submission."

"Thanks for the monologue, asshole." A new voice came from the top of the crater, and Rachel whirled around as Billy vaulted the edge on his mountain bike. He pedaled furiously down the slope and flung himself over the handlebars at Morrison, catching the stunned elf around the midsection with a perfect tackle. Elf and boy tumbled over each other in the dirt until they came to a stop at the edge of the portal with Billy astride Morrison. He punched the elf in the face again and again until Morrison's head lolled to the side, unconscious.

Billy stood up, dusting the rocks and dirt off his pants and looked around. "Now how do we stop this whole dragon apocalypse? Cause I've seen *The Walking Dead*, and I think dragons might be way worse than zombies."

"The portal has been weakened by my blood. Even if it is not opened today, it must be closed again permanently. That can only be done with blood."

"Okay, well, I vote we use the elf for a donor," Billy said, prodding Morrison's unconscious form with his foot.

"We must have the blood of all three species to re-seal the portal. We need human, elf, and dragon." Auros shook his head as he spoke.

"Well, here you go." Billy pulled out his pocketknife and slashed open his palm. He flicked his bleeding hand toward the portal, which flashed with a blinding light as the drops of his blood struck it. "Human blood. Now we toss the elf in, and we're good to go."

"Or I throw you and my idiot son into the portal and open it once and for all," Morrison said, leaping to his feet.

"I don't think so," Auros said, his sword flashing across the open space between them and cutting a line across Morrison's chest. The dragon waved his hands in similar intricate gestures as the motions Morrison used to open the portal and kicked the elf backward through the glowing rift. The portal flashed white, and the barrier obscuring the dragons shifted back to a milky-white.

"Now I must go through the portal to seal it," Auros said. "The spell I wove is different from the original spell. It will keep the dragons imprisoned forever, but at a cost. The magic that keeps the elves alive will vanish, as will all the old magics. You will no longer be able to call fire, Rachel, and your healing touch will fade in time as well. Once I pass through the portal, you must heal Scott as quickly as possible, or you will not be strong enough to fully mend his wounds."

"But…do you have to go?" Rachel asked, looking up at the handsome dragon. She was surprised to see a sheen of moisture in his eyes.

"I must. This world is no longer one of magic, but one of men. And men cannot live alongside magic any longer. I must go, but please remember me."

Rachel crushed herself to Auros' chest and wrapped her arms around him. "Forever. I promise."

Auros stepped back and bowed to Ben and Scott. "You were brave warriors. I am proud to call you friend." He turned to Billy, who looked away. "You learned the error of your actions and redeemed yourself. You proved yourself a true warrior." Then the teen shimmered into his true dragon form and dove through the portal. The colors in the rift flared once more, then a blinding flash exploded over the mountain, and it was gone.

EPILOGUE

Rachel stood for a moment staring at the place where the dragon had been, and then Scott moaned from the ground in front of her. She knelt beside him, placing her hands on his midsection. She closed her eyes and *reached* for the power, feeling her connection to the magic become more tenuous by the moment. She felt the tingle as the magic flowed through her hands and opened her eyes. Her hands were glowing with a warm yellow light, and the gaping wounds in Scott's abdomen knit themselves closed.

His eyes fluttered open, and he looked up at Rachel with a smile. "Nice wakeup call. Am I dead? 'Cause you look like an angel."

She laughed and sat back on her heels. A wave of exhaustion washed over her, and she almost fell over. Billy stepped over and put his hands on her shoulder to help steady her, and Scott's eyes flashed.

"What the hell are you doing here? This whole mess is your fault!" Scott tried to sit up, but his face paled, and he collapsed back flat. "That wasn't a good idea."

"Are you still hurt?" Rachel said, her voice weak.

"No, just really, really tired. I guess coming back from the dead takes it out of me."

"Yeah, bringing you back from the dead wasn't the easiest thing

I've ever done, either." Rachel reached over and put a hand on Scott's knee. "Scott…your dad, he…"

"I know. I wasn't totally out of it. Billy came back, decided to work on the side of the angels, saved all our bacon, and Auros and my dad went through the portal to seal it forever."

"Yeah, pretty much." Rachel looked away as a tear rolled down one cheek.

"It's okay, Rachel. I'll miss the scaly guy, too," Scott said from the ground. "But for now, could somebody help me up? I got rocks poking me in places I didn't know I had places."

Billy reached down and pulled Scott to his feet, then both boys helped Rachel stand. The trio slowly made their way to the top of the crater, then Rachel paused.

"Where's my dad?" she asked, looking around.

A horn honked from off to their right, where Ben stood beside one of the mine's king cab pickups. "You kids want a ride? I hear saving the world can make you tired."

They made their way down to the waiting pickup. As Rachel got into the truck, she thought for a moment that she saw a flash of gold dart across the sky, but when she blinked, it was gone.

STAY IN TOUCH!

If you enjoyed this book and would like to read more of my stuff, you can sign up for my mailing list! This link will let you stay on top of everything I'm doing, everywhere I'm going, and all my new releases! Sign up now and get a free ebook!
http://eepurl.com/fV4In

ACKNOWLEDGMENTS

Thanks as always to Melissa Gilbert for all her help, and for trying in vain to teach me where the commas go.

Many thanks to the amazing Natania Barron for this cover. You should go buy her new book, Wothwood. It's badass.

The following people help me bring this work to you by their Patreon-age. You can join them at Patreon.com/johnhartness.

Sean Fitzpatrick
Noah Sturdevant
Mark Ferber
Andy Bartalone
Nick Esslinger
Sharon Moore
Wendy Taylor
Sheelagh Semper
Charlotte Babb
Wendy Kitchens
Andrew Bolyard
Darrell Grizzle
Larry Nash

Delia Houghland
Douglas Park, Jr.
Travis & Casey Schilling
Michelle E. Botwinick
Carol Baker
Leonard Rosenthol
Lisa Hodges
Patrick Dugan
Noella Handley
Butch Howard
Bob Dobkin
Robin Castellanos
Lars Klander
Vickie DiSanto
Jared Pierce
Jeremy Snyder
Candice Carpenter
Theresa Glover
Salem Macknee
Trey Alexander
Brian Tate
Jim Ryan
Andrea Judy
Anthony D. Hudson
John A. McColley
Melissa Cole
Mark Wilson
Dennis Bolton
Shiloh Walker & J.C. Daniels
Andrew Torn
Sue Lambert
Emilia Agrafojo
Tracy Syrstad
Russell Ventimeglia
Elizabeth Donald

Samantha Dunaway Bryant
Shael Hawman
Bill Schlichting
Steven R. Yanacsek
Scott Furman
Rebecca Ledford
Ray Spitz

FALSTAFF BOOKS

**Want to know what's new & coming soon from
Falstaff Books?**

**Join our Newsletter List
& Get this Free Ebook Sampler
with work from:
John G. Hartness
A.G. Carpenter
Bobby Nash
Emily Lavin Leverett
Jaym Gates
Darin Kennedy
Natania Barron
Edmund R. Schubert
& More!**

http://bit.ly/FalstaffEmail

ABOUT THE AUTHOR

John G. Hartness is a teller of tales, a righter of wrong, defender of ladies' virtues, and some people call him Maurice, for he speaks of the pompatus of love. He is also the best-selling author of EPIC-Award-winning series *The Black Knight Chronicles* from Bell Bridge Books, a comedic urban fantasy series that answers the eternal question "Why aren't there more fat vampires?" In July of 2016. John was honored with the Manly Wade Wellman Award by the NC Speculative Fiction Foundation for Best Novel by a North Carolina writer in 2015 for the first Quincy Harker novella, *Raising Hell.*

In 2016, John teamed up with a pair of other publishing industry ne'er-do-wells and founded Falstaff Books, a publishing company dedicated to pushing the boundaries of literature and entertainment.

In his copious free time John enjoys long walks on the beach, rescuing kittens from trees and getting caught in the rain. An avid *Magic: the Gathering* player, John is strong in his nerd-fu and has sometimes been referred to as "the Kevin Smith of Charlotte, NC." And not just for his girth.

Find out more about John online
www.johnhartness.com